INFERNO

INFERNO

Robin Stevenson

ORCA BOOK PUBLISHERS

Library and Archives Canada Cataloguing in Publication

Stevenson, Robin H. (Robin Hjørdis), 1968-
Inferno / written by Robin Stevenson.

ISBN 978-1-55469-077-0

I. Title.

PS8637.T487I57 2009   jC813'.6   C2008-907661-3

First published in the United States, 2009

Library of Congress Control Number: 2008942002

Summary: Dante is disillusioned with school and wishes she was able to be open
about her sexuality, but her new friends make life even more difficult.

Orca Book Publishers gratefully acknowledges the support for its publishing
programs provided by the following agencies: the Government of Canada through
the Book Publishing Industry Development Program and the Canada Council for the
Arts, and the Province of British Columbia through the BC Arts Council
and the Book Publishing Tax Credit.

Design by Teresa Bubela
Cover artwork by Getty Images
Author photo by David Lowes

ORCA BOOK PUBLISHERS
PO Box 5626, STN. B
VICTORIA, BC CANADA
V8R 6S4

ORCA BOOK PUBLISHERS
PO Box 468
CUSTER, WA USA
98240-0468

www.orcabook.com
Printed and bound in Canada.
Printed on 100% PCW recycled paper.

12 11 10 09 • 4 3 2 1

To my family

ONE

The sun is barely up, but the sky is already blue and cloudless. The cool morning air fills my lungs and I focus on the feeling of my feet hitting the ground, my muscles stretching, my heart beating. Running is the one thing that keeps me from going completely crazy, but today it's not working as well as it usually does. My brain isn't switching off. I run down street after street, past the green lawns, the matching beige houses, the triple garages, the suvs.

We lived in a big city until just over a year ago. We had a cool apartment in the heart of downtown, and I rode the subway everywhere. There was the massive library, six stories high with glass skylights everywhere, a park where I used to run along miles of tree-lined paths, and all kinds of funky used bookstores and antique shops and cafés. Then Dad got transferred halfway across the country—he does something incomprehensible that involves software and a lot of acronyms—and now here we are. The burbs.

The nearest city, the one we're technically a suburb of, is a depressing concrete sprawl. Not that it matters. With no subway, no busses—unless you walk practically to the highway and wait forever—and no driver's license, it's not like I can go anywhere.

I was almost fifteen when we moved, and it hasn't exactly been a smooth transition. At my old school, all my teachers loved me. At my new school? Not so much. Apparently what was seen as "independent thinking" back in the city is called "attitude" here. Last year would have been hell if it wasn't for Beth. She was in my homeroom, and we started to talk because we'd see each other out running all the time. Pretty soon, we were spending every spare minute together. I floated through the rest of grade ten without bothering to get to know anyone else. Then in June, Beth and her family moved away, and I was back to being alone. This summer has been one long sharp ache.

I slow down as I run past the high school. Glen Ridge Secondary School. GRSS. It's a squat, gray, two-level building, as new and as ugly as everything else around here. Since last year, someone has planted a row of trees along the edge of the field. They're spindly little things. None come up past my shoulder. Granted, I'm five foot eleven, but still. The trees just look kind of sad. Anyway, summer holidays are over. By lunchtime today, everyone will be butting out their cigarettes on the skinny trunks.

I glance at my watch. Less than three hours until I'm back inside.

When I get home I head straight to the bathroom and take a long shower, as hot as I can stand, with a blast of cold at the end. I dry myself off quickly and wrap myself in a towel. Mom's left one of her magazines on the counter, and I flip it open and start reading while I brush my teeth. I always have to read something: If the magazine wasn't here, I'd be reading the list of ingredients on the toothpaste tube or the directions on Dad's jar of athlete's foot powder.

Top Ten Tips for Looking Younger the article reads. I snort. Like I want to look younger than sixteen. But I keep reading anyway. *Tip 1: Laugh lines, frown lines... their very names give them away. Every time you wrinkle your forehead or crinkle your eyes, those little lines get one step closer to being a permanent part of your face. The good news? By keeping a serene countenance, you can avoid the aging effects of excessive facial expressions.*

I toss the magazine aside. Unbelievable. I can't believe my mom reads this crap. Oh wait—yes, I can. It's probably half the reason she's always nagging me about my appearance.

I wipe clean a patch of the steam-fogged mirror, and my blurred reflection scowls back at me. My dark hair falls to my shoulders in a wet shaggy mess. Maybe Mom's right: It's time for a new look. I rummage in the drawer until I find a pair of scissors; then I hold up one hank of hair and cut. Then another and another, until I'm standing in a drift of fallen hair and all that's left on my head is maybe half an inch of thick dark fuzz. Even half-wet, it's already sticking straight up.

This haircut, combined with my sixteenth birthday present, should guarantee an interesting first day of school.

I turned sixteen at the beginning of July. Beth had been gone for two weeks, and it was just beginning to sink in that she had truly, completely and permanently disappeared from my life. I couldn't stand it. Everything hurt, and I felt like crawling out of my skin.

I didn't feel like celebrating, but Mom lives for special occasions. She insisted on doing the whole sweet-sixteen thing—a big pink cake, sixteen candles, all that. It pretty much broke her heart when I flatly refused to invite anyone from school. In the end, Mom and Dad and I sat around eating the cake by ourselves. Dad kept giving me sympathetic glances from across the table, and I kept cramming more cake into my mouth so that I wouldn't have to talk. Happy birthday to me.

Mom's always trying to create these perfect teenage moments and give me the life that she always wanted. Whether or not it's what I want doesn't seem to matter.

Anyway, I'd only wanted one thing for my birthday and that was to change my name. I'd wanted to change it since I was a kid, but it wasn't until this year that my parents had finally agreed. Probably just as well, really. If they'd agreed when I was six, I'd be called Rufus, after our old neighbor's basset hound.

Mom had cried a little when she gave me the green light. "Emily's such a pretty, gentle name," she said. "It's so feminine."

I feel bad for my mother, in a way. She'd have been such a great mom for a different kid. Not that she's a bad mom for me, but I know it hurts her that I don't want the same things she wants. I've got to give her credit though: Even though it's a lost cause, she never gives up hope that I'll improve. Her outlook is relentlessly positive.

She may not understand me, but it's not like I understand her either. Despite all her fussing and the crap magazines she reads, she isn't someone you can just dismiss. Underneath it all, she's actually pretty smart. Sometimes I think she's stuck in some retro-fifties time warp, trying to be this perfect wife and mother, when really she should have been, I don't know…a cosmetic surgeon, maybe. Or a talk-show host or an interior designer. In her own way, she's ambitious. It's just that her ambitions all seem to involve me. I figure she needs more to manage than just my life and her kindergarten class.

Anyway, it's official. I am Dante E. Griffin. I kept Emily as a middle name, just to make Mom feel better. I needn't have bothered. She always calls me Emily anyway.

TWO

I pull on my favorite jeans and a navy hoodie and head downstairs with some trepidation. The trepidation, it turns out, is justified. My mother takes one look at my hair, and her face collapses. I can see her making this tremendous effort not to cry, twisting her mouth and wrinkling her forehead in a way that her magazine would definitely frown upon. If magazines could frown, and if frowning didn't cause wrinkles.

"Well," she says at last. "Emily. What have you done?"

"Isn't that fairly obvious?"

"But what were you thinking?"

I have no idea what I was thinking. "It was getting in my face," I say. "Driving me nuts."

I can see the muscles jump in her throat as she swallows.

"I've read that short hair is coming back in style this winter," she says at last.

Like I said—relentlessly positive. I stick a couple of slices of bread in the toaster and look up as Dad walks in. "Morning."

He raises one eyebrow and lowers it again. "You look different. Did you do something to your hair?"

"You could say that," Mom mutters.

I just grin at him. He grins back. "Well, you look terrific. Very striking."

Mom shakes her head like we're both completely hopeless and refills her mug from the carafe of coffee on the kitchen island. She doesn't eat breakfast. Actually, she doesn't eat much at all unless you count lettuce and cottage cheese. Mom was very overweight when she was a kid, like over two hundred pounds. I think that's why she's so hung up on appearances: She knows how unkind people can be. She's destroyed all the photos of herself as a child, which is possibly one of the saddest things I've ever heard, and she's terrified of getting fat again. When I pointed out once that she was kid a long time ago, she got all offended because she thought I was saying she was old.

I pop my toast out of the toaster, spread a thick layer of apricot jam on it and pour myself a glass of milk. Dad slowly pours shredded wheat squares into a bowl, picks out all the broken ones and spoons sugar on top. Mom adds some skim milk to her coffee. Then we all sit down in our show-home kitchen, surrounded by brand-new stainless-steel appliances and cherry-wood cabinets, and eat our various versions of breakfast in silence.

My old school was small and had a strong arts focus. I'd liked it there. Everyone was pretty friendly and the teachers were really passionate about their subjects. There were some cliques, I guess, but nothing rigid. You could move between groups pretty easily. The city had tried to close the school a couple of years ago and bus us all to a bigger school, but everyone got organized and protested, and in the end our school stayed open. I was starting grade nine at the time, and I was so relieved that I could stay.

Then Dad got transferred, and I had to leave anyway.

Glen Ridge Secondary School couldn't be more different. It's big and sterile and unfriendly, and the teachers all seem to be holding on for the day they can collect their pensions. And the kids...well. My first day here, I felt like I'd accidentally wandered onto a movie set. There they were, all the groups you see in teen flicks: the jocks, the cheerleaders, the brains, the Goths, the stoners, the skaters, the nerds. It was as if some casting director had hired them all and the costume department had dressed them for their parts. Not subtle.

I don't really fit anywhere. I'm a runner, but I hate team sports. I'm smart, but I don't care that much about my grades. I like some of the stoner kids, but I'm not into drugs. The cheerleaders remind me of my mother.

I don't know how I'm going to deal with school now that Beth's gone. I have a feeling I'll be spending a lot of time alone.

The day begins with double bad news. I pick up my schedule from the office and discover that Mr. Lawson, the English teacher who hated me in grade ten, is now teaching grade eleven English. We get to spend another year together. And to make it even worse, I have him for homeroom. The thought of me and Mr. Lawson beginning every day together depresses me.

The stupid thing is that I should like English. I love reading. I'm crazy for books. But that's half the problem, right there. Mr. Lawson can take a book I love and analyze it until it's as dead as the dissected rats in the biology lab.

He's a book-wrecker. I hate that.

I'm heading down the second-floor hallway to his classroom when someone steps right in front of me.

I step to one side. "Excuse *me*," I say, kind of sarcastically. I've never seen her before. And I'd have noticed her: Her hair is so fair it's almost white, and she's ghost pale. Plus there's something odd about her face. I stare for a moment before I realize what it is: She has no eyebrows. She's not punk or Goth or anything; she's wearing no makeup at all and she's dressed in ordinary faded jeans and a sweater, which makes the eyebrow thing even odder and more unexpected. Even with eyebrows though, she wouldn't quite blend in. I can't put my finger on it, but she's definitely not your usual GRSS student.

She gives me this weird, no-eyebrow smile and hands me a piece of paper.

I shove it in my pocket like I couldn't care less what it's about, and I keep walking until I get around the corner. Then I pull it out and smooth the creases. It's neon pink, with big bold letters in all caps, and it says: *WOOF, WOOF. YOU ARE NOT A DOG. WHY ARE YOU GOING TO OBEDIENCE SCHOOL?*

I'm not sure whether to be insulted or amused.

THREE

Mr. Lawson doesn't look particularly pleased to see me. He gives me a cool nod when I walk in. "Emily," he says.

"Actually, I changed my name this summer," I tell him. "Legally. It's Dante now."

He gives a little snort, and my stomach starts to hurt.

Other kids drift in and take their seats. A couple of them nod at me; one asks how my summer was; most of them stare at my hair for a few seconds and then ignore me. One asks me, all phony innocence, where Beth is. Pretending to be friendly. It's not like I don't know about the rumors. I doodle an elaborate picture of Geryon, the monster of fraud, on the front cover of my binder. He's one of the creatures from Dante's *Inferno*, which is possibly my favorite book of all time. I draw Geryon scaled and hairy and give him a long serpent's tail with a venomous forked tip. Then I sit and wait for class to begin.

Mr. Lawson seems very pleased with himself. We are going to be doing a novel study, he tells us, and he's giving us three books to choose from. It's like he's doing us a huge favor: he is Giving Us A Choice. Granted, there aren't a lot of choices at GRSS, but still. Hardy, Dickens or Steinbeck. Three books by three dead white men. Three books I'd already read, or at least started to read. I have trouble conjuring up the expected gratitude.

When everyone puts up their hands to say which book they want, I just sit there and say nothing.

Mr. Lawson folds his arms across his chest. "What seems to be the problem, Emily?"

This is how he talks. Not *What's up?* or *What's wrong?* or even *What's the problem?* No. *What seems to be the problem?* Like without even asking, he can somehow tell it doesn't even qualify as a real problem. It only *seems* to be one.

On top of that, he's got my name wrong.

"It's Dante," I remind him. "Not Emily."

"Right," he says. He kind of drags it out—*riiiiight*. Long, slow and dripping with sarcasm: He's totally mocking me in front of the whole class. "So...*Dante*...what seems to be the problem?"

"I've already read those books," I say. "Can I pick something else? Um, please?"

He raises his eyebrows. "You've read all three? Even the Steinbeck? Somehow I doubt that."

I don't say anything. It's hard to know what to say really. Last year, conversations with Mr. Lawson usually ended with me getting sent to the office.

"Well?" Lawson says. His eyebrows are twitching and hovering in the vicinity of his receding hairline.

"Well what?"

"Well...*Dante*...which book are you going to read?"

I shrug. "Well...*Mr. Lawson*...I guess if I'm re-reading something, I'll take the Thomas Hardy. *Tess of the D'Urbervilles*." I'd read it last spring, before Beth left and before I got all obsessed with Dante Alighieri. "At least it has some exciting moments. Dead babies and murder and a hanging, you know?"

I guess that's a bit of a spoiler, but I want Lawson to know I've really read it. A couple of kids snicker. Lawson gives me a narrow-eyed look but drops the topic. He rattles on about the assignment, but I can't concentrate. I feel like throwing something through the window and running from the room. Running as far away as possible. I don't know how I'll be able to stand a whole year of this.

Less than ten minutes later he calls me Emily again. I know he's got a lot of names to remember, but give me a break. Last year, two teachers at our school changed their names: Miss Creston became Mrs. Hicks, and Ms. Barkley became Ms. Johnson. Personally, I think it's weird that some women still change their names when they get married—like, aren't we kind of beyond that whole deal? But the point is, I bet Mr. Lawson remembers *their* new names.

"It's Dante," I say again. "Not Emily."

Mr. Lawson leans back against his desk.

"Riiiiight." He smoothes his mustache. He does that all the time. It's one of those perfectly trimmed, TV-cop mustaches. He puts his hands in his pockets and sighs. "I suppose you're going to tell me you've read Dante's *Inferno* too."

Actually, I've read quite a lot of the *Divine Comedy*. The *Inferno* is the best part. I skipped over most of *Purgatorio* and a fair bit of *Paradiso*. Let's face it, hell is more interesting than heaven. It's kind of heavy reading, but I guess you'd expect that from a seven-hundred-year-old epic poem. It took me half the summer, and that was with the help of Cliff's Notes. But Lawson's not going to believe me anyway, so I just shrug.

He raises his eyebrows. "So why Dante then?"

Like it's any of his business. "That's personal."

"Riiiiight," he says again.

I'm not telling him the real reason, not in front of the whole class. Not a chance. It'll sound hokey, and I don't want to be laughed at.

Lawson waits, arms folded across his chest. Some kids shift in their seats to stare at me.

Screw it. If he wants an answer that bad, I'll make one up especially for him. "You really want to know?" I say quietly. "Fine. Dante's *Inferno* is about hell, right? And since

I apparently have to spend an eternity in school, which is basically hell on earth—"

"All right," he snaps. "That's enough. I suggest you get to work...Emily."

I lift my chin and meet his gaze straight on. "That's not my name," I say. "I legally changed it. I won't answer to Emily."

There is a hush in the class. No snickers. Everyone is waiting to see what's going to happen, hoping that Mr. Lawson will lose it and provide some entertainment, or at least waste a few more minutes of class time.

Mr. Lawson sighs. "Is this really the way you want to start a new year?"

"I haven't done anything," I say. "It's not my fault you don't like my new name."

"I had hoped that your attitude would have improved." He glances at the clock. "Not even nine thirty and already you're causing trouble."

I don't say anything.

"I think you better go and have a word with Mrs. Greenway," he says.

I stand up and leave the room.

I am halfway to the office when I see the no-eyebrows girl again. She's standing outside the main doors, smoking. I am half tempted to push the door open and ask what her note meant, but Mrs. Greenway spots me and beckons.

"Dante. Already?"

Mrs. Greenway is fifty-ish and extremely fat, with masses of gray- and brown-streaked hair and bright pink lipstick. Despite this, she's all right. She's one of the more reasonable people at GRSS.

I step into her office. "Hi, Mrs. G. Mr. Lawson sent me."

"Mm-hmm." She waits.

"Well, the thing is, he wanted to know why I changed my name."

She smiles. "I got your parents' letter. I've been wondering that myself."

"I just liked the name." I flop down in the big comfy chair that she's managed to cram into the corner of her office. "Emily was too...I don't know. It wasn't me."

"Dante's a great name. Knowing you, I'm assuming there's a literary allusion. You know who Dante was?"

"Sure. Italian poet. One of the greatest writers ever."

She smiles and squeezes herself into her desk chair. "Have you been reading the *Divine Comedy?*"

I nod. "I read a bunch of stuff this summer."

"And what was it that impressed you so much that you chose his name?"

I hesitate. What I'd said to Mr. Lawson wasn't quite true. School was hell, but that wasn't the reason I chose the name. "I liked what he said," I tell Mrs. G. "You know, about how we need to take responsibility for the world. As individuals, I mean. He said, 'If the present world go astray, the cause is in you, in you it is to be sought.'"

I shrug. "It's just cool, that's all. I mean, he wrote that like seven hundred years ago, you know?"

"Ahh. I do know." She smiles. "Yes, very cool indeed."

The word *cool* sounds funny coming from her, like it isn't something she would normally say. We sit in silence for a moment. Then Mrs. G. sighs. "I take it that isn't what you said to Mr. Lawson."

I squirm. It does seem a bit childish now. "No. I told him I picked it because of the *Inferno*. That school was hell, you know, and that since I was stuck here…"

"Oh dear."

"Yeah." There is a pause. For a second, I think she is going to ask me about Beth, but of course she doesn't. I don't imagine she pays too much attention to student gossip, and even if she had heard something, she probably wouldn't bring it up. It's weird, but I don't think I'd mind. I can almost imagine talking to her about Beth. Almost.

"Oh dear," she says again. She looks at me thoughtfully. "You usually have more sense."

"He kept calling me Emily. And he called me a liar."

She raises her eyebrows. "Really?"

"I said I'd already read the books he assigned, and he didn't believe me."

"Ahh."

Even though she's never said it, I have a feeling she doesn't like Mr. Lawson either.

Finally she sighs. "You haven't written a paper on these books before though?"

"No."

"So you can do the assignment."

"I guess."

She glances at her watch. "There's only ten minutes left of this period. Why don't you take a walk, then head on to your next class."

"Okay."

"And Dante…next time, maybe you could think before you speak. Some things are better kept to yourself."

I nod and leave the office. A couple of pink squares of paper lie on the hallway floor. I pick them up and study them for a minute. Apparently I'm not the only one that got the weird *Woof, woof* note. I open the main doors, step out into the bright sunshine and look around. Smoke still lingers in the air, but the no-eyebrows girl is gone.

FOUR

Mom and Dad usually get home pretty soon after me. Mom is teaching full-time for the first time since I was born. The little kids adore her.

I run all the way home, go straight up to my room and turn on my computer to send Beth a message. *How was your first day back, mine sucked, blah blah blah.* It doesn't matter what I write, because I'm not going to send it.

When Beth told me she was moving, I hadn't kidded myself that we'd stay close. Two thousand miles is a long way, and while computers and phones are great, they're also pretty limited. Even when Beth was here, she wasn't a big talker. Still, I figured we'd at least stay in touch. Tell each other what we were up to, who we were hanging out with, what movies we'd seen, stuff like that.

For a few days after she left, I sent her long e-mails telling her how much I missed her and talking about how much GRSS was going to suck without her there.

She didn't reply. I figured she didn't have her computer set up yet, so I waited a couple of days. Then I noticed that she'd updated her Facebook profile. So she was back online. I poked her a couple of times and sent her some virtual fish for her virtual aquarium. But I didn't hear from her, and it gradually began to sink in.

She wasn't going to write back. Not ever.

I stare at the computer screen and hold down the backspace key, erasing my e-mail to Beth one letter at a time. I wonder if she even thinks about me anymore. I log in to Facebook. I keep expecting to find that she's deleted me from her Friends list, but she hasn't yet. Maybe she just hasn't got around to it. Or maybe it hasn't occurred to her that I'd be checking her profile to see what she's doing. She doesn't write much, but she changes her status every day or two. Right now, it reads: *Beth is listening to cool tunes.*

It's pathetic. I feel like a cyber-stalker.

Mom knocks and opens my door without waiting for a response.

"Do you mind?" I say. "Maybe if my door is closed, it's because I actually want privacy. What if I was getting changed or something?"

She just laughs and walks across the room toward me. "Sorry. What are you doing?"

I close the window before she can see what's on the screen. "Nothing."

"Oh." She is quiet for a moment. "How was your day?"

"Fine. I guess. Mr. Lawson's a dickhead but whatever.

Apparently it's not a problem if a teacher can't be bothered to remember a student's name."

"I'm sure he means well."

She says this about absolutely everyone. She thinks the Pope means well, despite the fact that he's a complete idiot who thinks using birth control is, like, evil. Whatever.

"Are you making any friends?" she asks. "Since Beth left you don't seem to talk to anyone."

"That's because all the girls in my class are obsessed with stupid celebrities, Mom."

She sighs. "It isn't right that you spend so much time alone."

"Yeah, well. There are plenty of things worse than being alone." Like wasting my time talking about tabloid gossip.

"You're okay though? Right?"

"I'm fine."

She drives me crazy. I know she means well, to borrow her own phrase. Really, she's not a bad parent or anything. She loves me. It's just that because she loves me, she thinks she owns me. She thinks that she should be able to dictate and control everything about my life. All in my own best interests, of course.

Between school and my parents, there isn't a single square inch of my life that is really, truly my own. The only time I feel even remotely free is when I'm running. And for some reason, that gets me thinking about the no-eyebrows girl and the weird notes she was handing out today. Obedience school. Sit. Stay. Don't get up until the bell rings. Woof, woof.

I have to admit, she has a point.

The next day, I look for the girl when I get to school. I don't really expect to see her, but there she is, standing outside, wearing a thick multi-colored sweater and tight jeans.

I walk over to her. "Hi."

She grins at me. "Hi."

Up close, her eyes are pale blue. Sled-dog eyes. "So..." I feel off balance all of a sudden. "I was just wondering..."

"Wondering's good." She's holding a stack of papers, and she peels one off to hand to me. Lime green. Two identical buildings are roughly sketched on it and underneath, in all caps, it says: *HIGH SCHOOL. JAIL. CAN YOU SPOT THE DIFFERENCE?*

I raise my eyebrows. "That's a bit extreme, don't you think?"

She grins again. She has skinny cheeks and a wide mouth that's too big for her face and those weird pale eyes, but there's something about her face that is hard to look away from. She's kind of pretty in a fragile, no-eyebrows way.

"Think about it," she says. Her voice is husky and surprisingly low for someone so small. Nothing fragile about it. "Rules about where you can go and when. Asking permission to speak. Scheduled time each day to go out into the yard. Punishments if you don't do what you're told." She shrugs. "That's fucked up."

My mouth is probably hanging open. She's pretty much summed up how I've been feeling lately. I nod slowly and for some reason—don't ask me why, I never shake hands with people—I hold out my hand. "I'm Dante."

"Parker." Her hand is dry and warm, almost hot. "Good to meet you."

"You don't go to this school, right?"

"No. Thank Jesus. This has got to be one of the weirdest schools I've ever—"

I cut her off. "I know. It's bizarre."

"It's unreal."

"I know. I know."

"It's like something out of the movies," she says.

"I know! I mean, everyone's walking around like they're auditioning for a part."

Parker nods. "The cheerleaders, the jocks, the nerds…"

It's like she's been reading my journal. "I was so blown away by it all when I started here," I tell her. "Now I've simplified it to the Elites, the Athletes, the Academics, and the Deviants."

"Hah." She grins appreciatively. "So where do you fit in then?"

"I don't." I grin back at her. "What school do you go to?"

"I don't believe in school."

"You don't believe in it." I repeat her words flatly. It hadn't occurred to me that school was something in which I could or could not believe. Like fairies or Santa Claus or God.

"I mean, as an institution. I don't support it."

"So what are you doing here? I mean…" I nod at her stack of lime green papers.

Parker lights a cigarette and offers me the pack.

I shake my head. "I don't believe in supporting tobacco companies."

She laughs, lights up and watches me through a veil of smoke. "I'm trying to make people think, that's all. I visit different schools."

"You mean…"

"Hand out flyers, hang around, talk to people. People who are open-minded enough to question things." She waves her cigarette in the direction of the school doors. "People who haven't had every last spark of curiosity stomped out by years of education or incarceration or whatever you want to call it."

I feel a prickle of irritation. She is a bit too sure of herself. Like she thinks anyone who is still in school is an unthinking idiot. It's just not that simple. I mean, what choice do I have? "So how's it going then?" I ask. "Are many people interested?"

"Some are. Most aren't."

The bell rings. Through the glass doors I can see a rush of kids milling down the hallway toward their classrooms. "I guess I'd better go," I say.

"Up to you."

I look at Parker. She waits, non-eyebrows raised, and I wonder if she shaved them off. "Nah. I don't skip classes. Not worth the hassle," I tell her.

"Like I said, up to you."

I start to walk away. Then I turn back. "You really don't go to school? How old are you anyway?"

"Sixteen."

"And your parents? I mean…did they freak out?"

"Yeah, pretty much." She looks down at her hands. Her nails are short and ragged-edged. "You'd better go," she says. "If you're going."

"Yeah. See you around."

"Maybe." She turns her head and blows a cloud of smoke away from me. "Usually it doesn't take long for them to kick me off the school grounds."

For some reason, the thought that I might not see her again bothers me. A group of kids pushes past me, and I find myself still hanging back.

Parker laughs. "Tempted, are you? Thinking about a jailbreak?"

My next class is with Mr. Lawson. Another hour of being called Emily and being publicly accused of lying. Just thinking about it makes me want to run as far and as fast as I can. "Yeah," I say. "Screw it."

"You up for a drive?" she asks.

"I guess. Where to?"

"Tell you when we get there."

I make a face at her, exasperated, but she just laughs and I'm too curious not to go. "Fine," I say. "Whatever."

Parker's car is a total beater. An ancient Honda Civic that used to be blue and is now mostly rust colored. It has a tape deck instead of a CD player. I buckle up and Parker turns on the radio. Some guy with a British accent is interviewing a woman about terrorism.

"You can't trust the media," Parker says. "Most of it's just a bunch of lies to keep us in line."

"Us?"

"Everyone," she says darkly. "To make sure we do what we're told and don't ask too many questions."

I think about that for a minute. "What about nine-eleven though? I mean, you can't say that didn't happen."

Parker looks sideways at me, pale eyes unblinking. "Who knows who did it or why. I don't trust what we're being told, that's all."

"Well, there's no way everyone can be lying."

She rolls down her window and sticks her arm out to signal a left turn. "Sure, but how do you know who is?" She turns on to the highway, speeds up and switches the radio to a station playing some old, heavy metal song.

I suck on my bottom lip and watch Parker's profile out of the corner of my eye. I wonder where the hell we are going and why I am skipping class to hang out with a crazy girl with no eyebrows. Then I wonder why it feels so alarmingly good.

FIVE

Parker drives fast and taps her hands against the steering wheel, totally offbeat to the music. She is wearing fingerless black gloves, thin wool ones that are frayed at the edge. She has the longest skinniest fingers I've ever seen. Spider hands.

Eventually she takes an exit, makes a couple of turns and pulls into a parking lot.

I look at her quizzically.

"What do you think?" she asks.

"Of what exactly?" I look around, trying to figure out where we are.

Parker points at a large sign.

"Juvenile Detention Center?" I read out loud.

She turns to me with a wide grin. "Does it give you any ideas?"

"Umm..." I study the square gray building. "Not really."

"Okay, picture this: all the students at your school show up tomorrow morning, bright-eyed and bushy tailed with their sunny morning faces..." She pauses, watching me.

"And?"

"And there, right in front of the main doors, they see... this sign. Juvenile Detention Center."

I shrug. "So what. No one would care."

"Oh, come on. They would. You know they would. Just picture the looks on everyone's faces." She gives me a face-splitting grin. "It'd be great."

I grin back reluctantly, imagining everyone milling around, the air thick with *oh my gods*. The academics would disapprove; the elites and the athletes probably wouldn't get it. The deviants...well, they're a mixed group. Goths and nerds and stoners and a few unclassifiables: they're harder to predict. Mr. Lawson is easy though. He'd just stroke his mustache before tapping his heels together and disappearing off to the office to report it.

I can't help laughing. "Okay," I concede. "It's a pretty funny thought."

She brushes that aside. "Yeah, but it's more than that, right? Wouldn't it make them stop and think? Maybe realize that it's not so far off to call a school a detention center?"

I consider it. "I don't know," I say slowly. "Maybe. But I don't think most people would really think about it that much. I mean, look at the flyers you handed out."

"What about them?"

"Well, what did they accomplish?"

Parker's lips part in a slow, wide grin. "You're here."

"Yeah, but…"

She leans toward me, her voice low and intense. "That's how change happens, Dante. One person at a time."

A strange tingle runs down my spine. I swallow and try to stay cool. "I guess." Her eyes hold mine and I give in. "Okay. Okay. It'd be pretty cool."

Parker whoops and holds up a hand for a high five. "I knew you'd be game."

"Me? I said it'd be cool; I didn't say I'd *do* it."

She shrugs like she doesn't much care either way.

The wooden sign looks very solid and heavy. It is maybe four feet long and two feet high, and it sits low to the ground in the middle of a bunch of shrubs and flowers.

"It'd weigh a ton," I say. "I don't think it'd even fit in your car."

Parker rolls down her window, lights a cigarette, inhales and blows the smoke outside. She keeps her arm hanging out the window, and I watch the smoke curl upward into the still air. "That's okay. I've got a couple of other friends who will help."

"Oh. Well, good." I feel a bit hurt, which is stupid, but I'm not going to risk getting a criminal record just for a few laughs.

She pushes her white-blond hair away from her face and tucks it behind her ear. "I wish you were coming too. I'm sick of being the only girl."

"Maybe another time," I say. It sounds lame and we both know it.

Parker drops me a block from my house, right around the time I usually get home from school. I check for messages, in case someone has called to tell my parents I cut class, but there are none.

Which is good, because Mom would flip.

I head up to my room and turn on my computer. Beth hasn't sent me any messages. It's been three months; I'm crazy to think she still might. I log on to Facebook, click on Beth's profile and stare at her picture on the screen. Two thousand miles away, she must be sitting at her computer too. She changed her status just a few minutes ago. Now it reads *Beth loves her new school.*

I stare at her picture on the screen. It's an old photo; one I know well. I took it last summer. She's standing at the end of my driveway, wearing a tank top, running shorts and sneakers. She's laughing—openmouthed, head thrown back. Her teeth are Hollywood white, her slight overbite pushing her upper lip forward, her eyes dark slits, a long dimple curving in her left cheek.

I wonder if it means anything at all that she's still using a photograph I took. Probably not. I write a long message to her, telling her all about how Mom is driving me crazy, and about my haircut, and about Mr. Lawson and Parker. I tell her how much I still miss her and how I think about her every single day. Then I delete the whole thing before I'm tempted to hit Send.

Clearly, Beth has already moved on. I wish I could.

"How was school?" Mom asks at dinnertime. "Good day?"

I hate it when people ask questions like that—when they give you a little prompt to tell you what your answer should be. Mom does it all the time. I guess she'd rather avoid the truth if it isn't what she wants to hear.

"Sure," I say. "Good day."

Mom is short and fine-boned, with fair hair and brown eyes. It's hard to believe we are related. I'm definitely my dad's kid though. I have his wiry dark hair—now cut the same as his, come to think of it—his tall, broad-shouldered build and his blue eyes.

I have my dad's obsession with books and reading too. When I was little, he used to read to me all the time: *The Wind in the Willows, Peter Pan and Wendy, Alice's Adventures in Wonderland.* The original unabridged texts, never the Disney versions. When I was in first grade, we moved on to *The Jungle Book, Treasure Island* and *Gulliver's Travels.* Poetry too—T.S. Eliot, Edward Lear, Lewis Carroll. We memorized *The Hunting of the Snark* together. I used to spend hours reciting it to myself.

None of which really equipped me to deal with classmates raised on morning cartoons and after-school sitcoms. It was probably just as well that I'd also inherited Dad's loner tendencies.

"Anything interesting happen?" Mom asks, ever hopeful.

I think about my day. "Not really." *Unless you count*

cutting class and going to the Juvenile Detention Center with a girl with no eyebrows.

She starts dishing the bright orange soup. Clearly she is on a health kick again. I suspect one of her magazines is to blame for this rather toxic-looking dinner. Maybe it's supposed to make my hair grow faster.

"What are you up to this evening?" she asks. "Any plans?"

"Nope."

"Homework?"

"Some. I might just read."

"You read too much. You always have your nose buried in something."

"So? I like reading."

She presses her lips together. "It doesn't seem right. You're a beautiful girl, Emily. You should be going out with friends, buying clothes, talking about boys..."

She's unreal. "Mom, are we seriously having this conversation?"

"When I was your age, I'd have loved to go to parties and dances and all that."

"Right. Mom, I've been to parties, okay? Everyone plays drinking games and gets wasted. Then they either make out or have stupid boring conversations about nothing. I'm so not interested."

She looks a little shocked. "I'm sure not all the parties are like that."

"Yeah, well. Just be glad I'd rather read."

"Oh, honey. Of course I'm glad you like to read.

I just don't like to see you spending so much time on your own." She hesitates. "There's a course I was looking at…"

"Really? You're going to do a course?"

"No, no. For you."

I should have guessed. "What kind of course?" I ask.

"It's a…well, a social thing. A group for girls." She shifts in her chair and looks at Dad instead of me. "Self-esteem. Social skills. That kind of thing."

Dad looks at me, eyebrows gathered and forehead wrinkled. "First I've heard," he says apologetically.

I ignore him and glare at Mom. "Please. My self-esteem is fine. My social skills are fine."

"Of course they are, sweetie. I just thought it might be a good way for you to make some new friends."

"Yeah. If I wanted friends with low self-esteem and poor social skills, I'm sure it'd be terrific."

"Emily…"

"I'm going up to my room." I push away my orange soup and stand up. "To be anti-social in private."

Upstairs, I lie on my bed for a while. I check my e-mail. I do a hundred sit-ups and fifty push-ups. The big old-fashioned clock on my wall ticks away loudly. I wonder if Parker and her friends are going to steal the sign tonight. I realize I never got a phone number from her. I don't know her last name or where she lives.

For some reason, this makes me feel horribly depressed.

I get up and go down to the basement. Dad is setting up a miniature historic battle of some kind, meticulously arranging hundreds of tiny painted figures on a large land-scaped table.

I touch the smooth hard surface of a lake. "Cool. How'd you do that?"

"Epoxy." He glances at me. "Don't touch it; you'll leave fingerprints."

"No I won't." I wipe the surface with my sleeve. "Is Brad coming over?"

"Later. Yeah."

Dad's friend Brad lives a few blocks away, in a house that is absolutely identical to ours. Once a week or so, they get together and play these war games until about three in the morning. It's a little weird, but I guess it's something to do.

"Dad? This course Mom wants me to take…"

"Mmm."

"Can you, like, talk her out of it?" I know it's hopeless but I have to try.

"Oh. Well. You know, when your mom gets set on something…"

"Yeah, but…"

He frowns. "Maybe she'll forget. If it's just a passing thought, you know, it might be better not to mention it."

He just doesn't want to argue with her. He hates conflict. Most people wouldn't consider a slight difference of opinion to be conflict, but he does. He's a wuss.

I pick up a little soldier and pretend to examine him closely. "Okay, I won't mention it."

Dad frowns again. "Make sure you put him back in the same place."

I sigh, put the soldier back and head upstairs. Mom's sitting on the couch watching TV. She pats the couch beside her. "Come and watch with me."

I shake my head. "I'm going for a run."

The rhythm of my feet against the smooth road calms me. I run past a hundred identical houses, head into the next subdivision over and run past a few hundred more. Thousands of houses that all sprang up at once, a virtual forest of conformity that stretches all the way to the highway. Surely it wouldn't have been that much more work to vary them a little. Although we do seem to have one of the few houses with no pool. If I have to be stuck here, a pool would have been nice.

Dante Alighieri should have designated a special circle of hell for the builders who designed this place.

I think about Dante's *Inferno* a lot. It's funny, because it's all about the afterlife, and my family isn't at all religious. My dad says he's a humanist, and my mom says she believes in some kind of higher power but not in heaven or hell. As for me, I've been an atheist since I was about eight. There's something appealing about Dante's vision though: everything laid out so neatly, a circle of hell designed for every kind of sinner, the punishment tailored to fit the crime.

The builders should be sentenced to an eternity in the suburbs. Backyard barbecues with Jell-O salads and pineapple cheese bakes. Bumper stickers that say *Support Our Troops* and *I heart my honor student.* Inground sprinklers in every lawn, all controlled by a central unseen switch. Stepford wives at every front door.

I slow down, thinking of Parker and how she'd echoed my thoughts about GRSS, right down to the high school movie idea. I wish I could tell her about Dante's circles of hell. I bet she'd like it.

S I X

When I arrive at school the next day, the first thing
I do is look around to see if Parker has brought the sign.
But there's nothing out of the ordinary happening. Just the
usual crowd of people hanging around, waiting for the bell
to ring. Pavlov's dogs, minus the drooling. I sigh and kick
a pebble along the asphalt.

"Hey."

I look up, hoping for a second that Parker has come
back. But it's just Linnea, one of my stoner acquaintances.
Closest thing I have to a friend now. "Hey."

"I loved what you told Mr. Lawson yesterday. About
your name? That was awesome." She giggles. "The look on
his face. Classic."

"I can't stand him."

"Me neither." Linnea flicks the ash from her cigarette
and shifts her weight from one foot to the other. "So, I heard
Beth moved away this summer. That's a drag for you, huh?"

"Yeah. Kind of."

"You two were pretty close, weren't you?"

There's something about her tone that suddenly makes me feel cautious. I shrug. "Well, we used to run together most days."

"Uh-huh." Linnea drops her smoke and grinds it under the heel of her boot. She is looking down, and her dark hair hangs forward, hiding her face so I can't see her expression. "I heard you guys were real close."

Mind your own business. "Are you getting at something, Linnea?"

She looks up at me, blue eyes wide and innocent, red lipstick dark against her pale freckled skin. "No. Just, you know. I guess you must miss her."

"Sure," I say flatly. "I miss her."

Linnea drops her eyes. She's too polite or too chicken to ask directly, but I guess she's heard the rumors too. The stupid thing is that there's no way anyone should know that me and Beth were more than friends. We never told anyone. It's just because we hung around together all the time and neither of us had a boyfriend. Then one day last spring, I passed her a note in class—nothing important; I can't even remember what it said—and that bastard Lawson intercepted it. "A love note?" he asked, sarcastically. Everyone laughed. That's all it took to get a rumor started.

I figure that's why Beth never wrote to me. She couldn't handle anyone knowing about us. She wanted to leave all that behind.

By Thursday, the sign from the juvenile detention center still hasn't appeared. I start to wonder if Parker and her friends have picked another school. There's no particular reason for them to bring it to GRSS. When I get home, I check the local paper, reading through carefully in case there are any reports of vandalism or theft on Tuesday or Wednesday evening. There's nothing.

Maybe it wouldn't be in the paper anyway.

I check for messages. None. Beth's updated her status again. *Beth has joined a running group.*

It figures. She was always more of a joiner than I am. Most people are. I liked running with Beth, but for me the idea of a group takes all the appeal out of running. To be honest, much as I miss Beth, I actually prefer running on my own. I kind of like to let my mind wander when I run.

Glad you're still running, I write. *GRSS still sucks. The teachers suck, the kids suck and the school feels like a prison.* I remember Parker's lime green papers: *School. Jail. Can you spot the difference?* I wonder what Beth would think of Parker. Probably she'd think she was crazy. Then, since I'm not sending the e-mail anyway, I let it all spill out. *I miss you so much. We were together almost a year— don't you miss me at all? How come you just disappeared? You could have written and told me it was over instead of letting me keep writing and waiting. I feel like an idiot, still thinking about you all the time. It's been three months now, so I guess I should get over it. I just don't understand though.*

There's still rumors about us at school, but it's old news now. No one really cares anyway, except you. Is that why you never wrote to me? Are you trying to pretend nothing ever happened between us?

I stop writing and stare at my words on the screen, imagining actually sending her this message. I wonder if she'd even read it or if she'd just delete it unopened. My fists clench, nails digging into my palms, and everything inside me feels clenched tight too; my jaw and chest and stomach ache. It's so hard to let go of her without even having a chance to say good-bye.

Mom has made another brightly colored soup for dinner. Green this time. It's very thick and rather slimy-looking.

Dad pokes it with his spoon. "Um, what is this, honey?"

"Okra, swiss chard, broccoli and cucumber soup," Mom says.

Okra. That would be the slime factor.

He takes a mouthful and swallows. I can see his Adam's apple bob up and down convulsively. "Delicious."

"It's high in free radicals," Mom says. "Or wait—are those the bad ones? Was it anti-radicals? Anyway, the ones that prevent cancer."

"Good, good." Dad fetches the salt shaker from the kitchen counter and dumps about a tablespoon of salt onto his soup.

Mom shakes her head but says nothing.

I taste mine. Gross. "Pass the salt, Dad?"

Mom looks at me. "Emily...sorry, honey...Dante?"

"What?" I shake salt on my soup before she can object.

"Ahhh...Dad and I were talking and we decided it would be a good idea for you to go to that group. You know, the one I mentioned the other night?"

My heart sinks. "Not the social skills thing."

She nods.

I glance at Dad. *Traitor.* I bet he didn't even try to talk her out of it. "Aw, no. That's crap. Really." I look across the table at Mom. "I've got friends, okay?"

"Well, *I've* never met them."

She hasn't met them, therefore I must not have any. *Oh wait, right, I don't.* "I'm fine, Mom. My social skills are stellar."

"Oh, honey. It's not a criticism of you. It's just...well, I remember how hard it was to always be on the outside, you know?"

I push my chair back from the table and stare at her. "Mom! I am NOT YOU, okay?"

Dad frowns at me. "Don't talk to your mother like that."

This is typical: Dad only seems like he isn't paying attention. Anytime I criticize my mother even slightly, he wakes up. I take a deep breath and lower my voice. "I am not you, Mom. I am not a social outcast. I am not getting bullied or left out or made fun of. So if you want to take your inner adolescent to a social skills class, be my guest. But leave me out of it."

"Actually, I signed you up already," she says. She meets my eyes nervously, her cheeks pink and eyes slightly wet. "Just give it a try, all right? If you don't like it after a couple of weeks, you can stop going. But I want you to try it."

I put my elbows on the table and rest my chin on my hands. There is zero point in arguing with my mother once she makes up her mind. She's steel. No, she's titanium. The tears are just another weapon in her arsenal, and they always defeat me. I can't stand to make Mom cry. "A couple of weeks? So I have to go twice?"

"At least twice," she says firmly. "The first session is tomorrow evening."

"Friday night? Seriously?" I shake my head in disbelief. "It's going to be a bunch of losers sitting around talking about being losers. You do realize that?"

"You're not a loser and you're going."

"Because you're forcing me to."

Mom blinks a couple of times and gives me a bright smile. "I bet you'll have fun," she says.

The next morning, I look for Parker at school, but she isn't around. The sign isn't there either. I wish I'd said I'd go and steal it with her.

Sitting at my desk is torture. I wonder what circle of hell this is and what I did to deserve it. Mr. Lawson drones on and on. I have restless legs. My knee bounces up and down like crazy, like there's too much energy inside me and stray sparks are shooting off everywhere, twitching my muscles. I feel bored and restless and impatient. I want something to happen.

So when Mr. Lawson calls me Emily again, I kind of lose it.

"You know, I'd like you to use my real name," I say. "It's not that much to ask."

"I'm terribly sorry." Total sarcasm. "Dante. As I was saying, if you could be so good as to share with the class your thoughts on the topic at hand..."

"*I'm* terribly sorry," I say, equally sarcastic. "I'm afraid I wasn't paying attention and I have no idea what the topic at hand was."

He strokes his mustache. I can tell he is totally enjoying this.

"Do you intend to pass this class, Miss Griffin? Because it seems unlikely if you don't start paying a little more attention."

I try to recall whether he has even said anything about class participation marks. "I thought we were graded on our papers and exams. Not our attentiveness."

The classroom was dead silent.

"Miss Griffin," he snaps. "I've had enough of your attitude. I suggest you discuss it with Mrs. Greenway down at the office."

I should stop, but I can't. "Why? Don't we have a right to know what our grades are based on? Because I don't remember seeing attitude mentioned on the course outline either."

"Miss Griffin." He stands up and steps toward me.

"I'll write a kick-ass paper," I say. "And I'll write a kick-ass exam too. Go ahead and fail me, but I'll be asking to have my grade reviewed."

Someone behind me draws a sharp breath and someone else stifles a nervous giggle.

Mr. Lawson's face turns red. "Get. Out. Now."

I stand up and face him. "I'm already gone."

Mrs. Greenway sighs when I walk in.

"Oh dear," she says. "Dante. What happened this time?"

I feel shaky. I sit down in the big chair and rest one ankle across my other knee. For a minute I don't say anything. Then I shake my head. "I'm not going back to that class."

She just waits.

"I hate it," I say. "He's a bully."

Mrs. Greenway pats her big hair thoughtfully. She takes off her reading glasses and lets them dangle from a cord around her neck. Then she looks at me and frowns. "So," she says, "what are you going to do?"

I don't say anything for a minute. English is a required subject. I wish Mrs. Greenway taught it. One whole wall of her office is lined with bookshelves. Mostly hardcover books about teaching and leadership, but some other stuff mixed in there too: Jane Austen novels; a whole bunch of books by George Orwell; Ray Bradbury's *Fahrenheit 451*, which I read at my old school and loved. "I don't know," I say at last. "I just don't want to be here anymore. Especially in that class."

"It's only the first week. It'll get better."

"Maybe. Maybe not. Maybe it'll get worse."

She sighs. "You are way too bright to even think about dropping out."

As if my parents would ever let me. "Isn't there another English class I could transfer to?"

"It's not that straightforward. If I switched students' classes every time someone complained about a teacher, it'd be chaos." Her mouth twitches a bit. "Well, you can probably imagine."

"Yeah. Mr. Lawson's class would be empty."

She says nothing, which I take to be confirmation. It helps to know I'm not the only one who can't stand him. "So I'm stuck with him?"

"I'm afraid so," she says. "What exactly happened in class?"

"Same old thing that happened all last year. He got on my case, I mouthed off."

"Can't you just...bite your tongue? Think what you want but keep it inside?"

"It doesn't seem to be one of my strengths, Mrs. G."

"It's only the first week, but you know, if things don't improve, there are alternatives. Maybe we should talk about them."

My heart is still racing from my argument with Mr. Lawson. I'm not in the mood to talk about anything. Mrs. Greenway rattles on about some other program, independent studies, self-directed learning, blah blah blah. It still sounds like school, and all I want is to be as far away from school as possible.

SEVEN

With all the crap at school, I manage to forget all about the stupid social skills group.

Unfortunately, Mom does not. She's done everything but pick out my outfit for me. Seriously. She's gotten me a little notebook and a new pen and packed me a snack like I'm one of her kindergarten students.

"Mom? I just had dinner. I don't need a snack."

She sighs. "I wish you hadn't cut your hair so short."

"Yeah, well. Too late now."

"Can't you at least wear something other than those old jeans? You know, you only get one chance to make a good first impression."

"Mom...," I say warningly.

"Okay, okay." She forces a smile. "Let's go."

I reluctantly follow her out to the car.

Mom unlocks the doors and gets in. "How are you feeling? Looking forward to it?"

I roll my eyes behind her back. "No, Mom. I wouldn't say that exactly."

She sighs again. "Well, try to have a positive attitude."

I buckle up my seatbelt, feeling trapped. I wonder what Mom would do if I said I wasn't going to go to school anymore. I mean, she can't make me go, right? If I just refused…Though I suppose she could make my life pretty miserable. I stare out the window and wish I were anywhere else.

Mom pulls into a parking lot. "I'll be back in two hours!" she says cheerfully.

The group meeting appears to be in the basement of a church. Mom hadn't mentioned that, probably because she knows how I feel about organized religion. I like churches about as much as I like schools. All these places where someone stands at the front of a room and tells everyone what they ought to think.

I don't bother waving. I trudge through the doors and down the stairs and into a small, brightly lit room. *Abandon all hope ye who enter here.* That's from the *Inferno.* It's the inscription on the gates of hell. In the poem, the first thing Dante sees when he passes through the gates are the Opportunists, the souls of people who didn't care about good or evil but were basically just out for themselves.

The first thing I see when I enter the room is a curly-haired woman in a flowered dress.

"Hello!" Her voice is so high it sounds like she's been sucking back helium. "And welcome! You're new, so you must be Emily."

"Dante," I say. "Dante Griffin."

Flowered Dress Woman frowns down at her clipboard. "That's funny...It says here..."

I ignore her. Because sitting there, along with half a dozen other girls, is Parker.

I don't get a chance to talk to her right away. Flowered Dress finally clues in that Emily Griffin and Dante Griffin are one and the same and ushers me over to the circle of girls.

"This is..." She breaks off, still a bit confused about who I actually am.

"Dante," I say firmly. "Hi."

No one says anything. I guess I shouldn't have high expectations given that I'm in Social Skills 101. But Parker winks at me from across the circle and flashes me a grin. She's wearing black today, and it makes her white-blond hair and fair skin look spooky pale. She sits with her legs crossed twice, knee over knee, one ankle tucked back behind the other leg. Her limbs look as thin and bendy as pipe cleaners.

Flowered Dress introduces herself as Shelley and says how *thrilled* she is to be here and what an *honor* it is to share in our *journeys*. I try not to throw up.

"Well," she says, slowing down as she finishes her spiel, "since we have a new member tonight"—big smile in my direction—"shall we start off with introductions?"

Silence from the group. Parker crosses her eyes at me.

"I'll start us off, shall I?" Shelley says.

She's just like my mother—giving a little prompt that tells you how to answer. But even with her cues, we are a dismal failure. We all say nothing.

"My name is Shelley," she says again, beaming at us. "I'm your group leader and I've been running this group for the last two years. I love my work, and I'm very happy to be here with you all."

Parker catches my eye and makes a gagging gesture.

Shelley pretends not to notice. "Jasmine, why don't you go next?"

A heavy girl with short blond hair sniffs loudly. "Uh, I'm Jasmine."

"And can you tell us a little about yourself, Jasmine?"

"Uh, like what?"

"Anything you would like to share." Shelley's smile hasn't even flickered yet. It's sort of impressive, in a creepy and slightly depressing way.

There is a long, long silence.

"Jasmine?"

"What?"

"Did you want to say anything else? About yourself?"

"No."

I look at my watch and blow out a long breath. Two minutes down, one hundred and eighteen to go. I glance at Parker, who is chipping off her pale blue nail polish with an expression of intense concentration. I wonder what the hell she is doing here.

When it is my turn to introduce myself, I say, "Hi. I'm Dante. I'm in grade eleven at GRSS." Then I look right at Parker. "Good to see you again."

Parker ignores the rest of the group. "Hey, Dante," she says. "I'd have called you, but I never got your number."

Shelley's smile is finally starting to wilt. "Parker, can you introduce yourself to the group? Please?"

"We'll talk at break," Parker says to me. "I've got something to tell you."

After the introductions, Shelley sets a bunch of flowers on a table in the middle of the circle.

"I've got a special opening exercise for us today," she says, fussing over the arrangement. "I think you'll like this one. And it'll help you all to get to know each other better."

I glance around the circle. There are seven of us: Parker, myself, the heavy sniffing girl called Jasmine, a thin dark-haired girl whose name I can't remember but whose mouthful of orthodontia (complete with head gear) explains her social problems, a redhead with a paisley bandana, a short-haired girl with dark eyes and brown skin, and a serious-faced girl with straight blond hair to her waist. Sylvie, Nicki and Claire, the last three are called.

"Now, everyone gets to choose a flower," Shelley says. "Dante, would you like to go first?"

I don't have a good feeling about this. What exactly are we going to do with the flowers? Some kind of art activity, maybe? I take the flower that is closest to me. It appears to be some kind of daisy.

Parker stands up next. She gazes at the flowers as if she is thinking deeply and takes a red rose.

One by one, the other girls each choose a flower. Then we all turn to Shelley to see what we are supposed to do next.

Her smile has recovered now that we are all blindly following her instructions. "I'd like you each to say a few words about why you chose the flowers you did...what does your choice say about who you are?"

Nicki snorts loudly.

Shelley ignores her and looks at me hopefully. "Dante? Would you like to start?"

I want to laugh, but I feel kind of embarrassed for Shelley, so I give her a lame smile. "Yeah, whatever." I glance down at my daisy. "I just took the closest flower. I didn't know it was supposed to mean something."

Shelley sighs.

Claire smoothes her long hair with one pale hand. "May I go next, Shelley? To help Dante understand how these exercises work?"

Across from me, Parker crosses her eyes. She pulls a petal off her rose, sticks it in her mouth and starts chewing slowly.

She's so beautiful. Sitting there, all in black, with that rose in her hand, she looks almost unreal. Like a photograph or a painting or an actress from an old movie. I just want to stare at her, but I drag my eyes away and look down at the flower in my hands. No doubt Parker is straight, but I think I might have a bit of a crush on her anyway.

I push the thought aside, twirl my daisy between my fingers and tuck it behind one ear.

Claire leans toward me, ignoring my daisy. "I chose the pansy because it hides its beautiful bright colors at its center. At first glance, it looks drab and dark. But if you take a closer look—if you take the time to get to explore it—then you see the amazing hues hidden within." She smiles at me. "See? I'm like that too. Once you get to know me. That's why I chose it."

"And 'cause she's a fucking pansy herself," Nicki informs me.

"Nicki. That's enough." Shelley's voice sounds sharp for a moment, almost confident; then her nervous manner returns. "Uh, Parker? How about you go next?"

Parker plucks another petal and eats it. "I love roses," she says. "Love 'em."

At the break Parker grabs my arm and pulls me outside. We sit down on a cold cement barrier in the parking lot and she lights a cigarette.

"Brutal, isn't it?"

I raise my eyebrows. "It's something, all right."

She exhales a cloud of smoke into the darkness.

I look at her curiously. "How come you're here? I mean, my mom made me come, but your parents don't even make you go to school."

"Yeah. I don't even live with them."

"Seriously?"

She shrugs. "Yeah. I have my own place."

"You do? Seriously?" I sound like an idiot but jeez. She's the same age as I am.

"Yeah. Well, with my boyfriend."

Boyfriend. It figures.

Parker holds her cigarette close to the webbed part of her fingers, so that her mouth is hidden by her hand every time she takes a drag. "I still see my parents every week though. We had this deal when I moved out—they help out with the rent and I have to keep seeing my counselor." She wrinkles her nose. "And my counselor wanted me to do this group."

I'm kind of surprised. I didn't think Parker let anyone tell her what to do. "I said I'd come twice," I tell her. "But that's it."

"It's not so bad. I mean, it's pretty lame, but, you know, whatever. Shelley's all right. She means well."

"God, Parker. You sound like my mother."

She laughs. Then she pulls a pen out of her pocket. "You have any paper? Give me your phone number. Jamie and I don't have a phone, but I'll call you."

I check my pockets, but I didn't bring any paper either.

Parker hands me the pen and holds out her arm, palm up. "Here. Just write it on my arm."

I steady her wrist with my left hand and write my phone number on the pale underside of her forearm. Her arm is thin and muscular, the blue veins visible through the skin. "You know that thing we talked about? Stealing that sign?"

"Sure."

"Have you done it yet? You know, with your friends?"

"No. We were talking about doing it Sunday night though." She grins at me, the corners of her mouth lifting to make two neat creases. "Did you change your mind, Dante? You want to come along?"

I hold my breath for a second. I've never really done anything like this. Not even close. I mean, I've never even shoplifted a chocolate bar or scrawled graffiti on a bathroom wall. So this is a bit of a leap.

"Come with me." Parker drops her cigarette butt on the ground. "Come on. It'll be fun."

I nod slowly. "Okay. I'll come."

"Awesome. I'll pick you up." She high-fives me; then she laughs. "I always figured you would. That day I met you, you know, when we talked about your school being like something out of the movies…"

"I know. I felt like you'd been reading my journal, it was so exactly what I thought."

She laughs again.

I feel all warm and relaxed, sitting here with her. I feel like Parker *gets* me, even more than Beth did. And the more I get to know her, the more I like her. "Hey, Parker?" I say. "I can't stand it at school. I mean, I've only been back there for a week, but it's hell. I feel like I'm wasting my life."

Parker nods. "That's the problem with making education mandatory. If you could study and learn what you wanted instead of what the state decides you should be programmed with..."

"Well, I'm sixteen. So technically it isn't mandatory, right? I could quit."

"Sure. But you've had, what, eleven years of school where you've had no say at all. Don't you think that is part of how you feel now? Like, that resentment just builds?"

"Maybe. But what about you? Why'd you drop out?"

"I didn't want to support a system I didn't believe in," she says.

"But..." I don't quite know what it is I need to ask. "What does it feel like, just to drop out?"

"I don't regret it," Parker says slowly. "But...well, lately I've been wondering what to do."

Shelley is calling us to come back in, but we ignore her.

"Are you thinking about going back to school?" I ask her.

Her face is pale in the dim glow of the streetlights. "Maybe. I don't see how I can, really." She sighs. "Don't say anything to Jamie, okay? If you meet him Sunday night."

"No. Course not. But...well, why would you go back?"

"I don't know. I probably won't anyway."

Shelley calls us again. Parker gets up. "We'd better go in before she has a stroke."

I follow her to the door and look down the stairs to the brightly lit room. "Another whole hour of this..."

"I hope she's brought more flowers. I'm still a little hungry."

I laugh, but inside I feel all churned up and unsettled.

I can't imagine telling my parents that I want to drop out.
I can just hear my mom. *Emily, don't be ridiculous. You don't
mean that, do you?* No, Mom. Of course I don't.

Parker skips lightly down the steps, and I follow. I'm
already trying to figure out how I'm going to get out of the
house to meet her on Sunday.

EIGHT

Shelley writes across the top of a sheet of flip-chart paper. All I can see is flowered fabric, because she is standing in the way, but I can smell the slightly dizzying fumes of permanent marker.

She stands back, points to her words and reads them aloud: "'When I have healthy self-esteem, I...'"

Beside me, Claire's hand shoots up.

Shelley ignores her. "How about we do this in a round? Each of us contributing one statement that feels true to us. I'll start. When I have healthy self-esteem, I believe in myself and my capabilities."

She writes down her own words and then she turns to me, and I make a mental note not to sit on her left-hand side next time. "Um. I feel good about myself?" Duh.

"Wonderful! Yes! When we have healthy self-esteem, we feel good about ourselves!" Shelley beams at me like

I'm a puppy who's just figured out how to shake a paw. I half expect her to hand me a dog cookie, but instead she just writes my words down and another wave of toxic fumes wafts in my direction.

Claire looks at me, and I can practically feel her resentment.

"Jasmine? Your turn." Shelley leans forward encouragingly.

"Me?" Jasmine shifts her bulk forward in her chair and sniffles some more. I can't tell if she has a cold or is sort of crying all the time. I hand her a Kleenex from a box on the table.

"Thanks." She keeps her eyes on the ground and picks at a scab on her arm.

The clock ticks. No one says anything. Jasmine just sits, breathing heavily. I'm feeling so anxious for her, it's crazy. I want to whisper the answers to her or tell her to just forget it. I can't stand it.

Finally she sighs. "Uh, I guess it's just like feeling good about yourself?"

Shelley purses her lips. "Well, yes. But that's what Dante said. Can you come up with something of your own?"

"It doesn't matter," I say quickly. "I mean, if that's what's true for Jasmine, shouldn't you just write it down?" *And give her a goddamn dog cookie too.*

Jasmine's eyes flick toward me for about a millisecond. I smile but not fast enough for her to see.

"Oh. Well, I suppose so." Shelley sounds irritated, but she writes it down a second time. "Nicki? You're next."

Nicki grins. "When I have healthy self-esteem, I feel good about myself."

Parker starts laughing, and Shelley lets out a long sigh from between tight lips. She looks at me, narrow-eyed, before she writes Nicki's response on the flip chart.

Great. I've instigated a rebellion. I'm already being seen as a troublemaker. Well, at least I'm used to it.

The flipchart is followed by another brainstorming exercise, then an art exercise and then a closing circle. Shelley reads a poem, which I stop listening to after the part about us all being children of God; then she says it's time for our closing circle.

"This is where we all join hands and sing 'Kumbaya,'" Parker tells me.

"Parker. Please." Shelley's cheeks are flushed, and I can't help wondering what this group is doing for her own self-esteem. "What I want to do today is for you each to say one thing…just one thing…that gets in the way of having healthy self-esteem."

This doesn't strike me as a very upbeat note to end on, but whatever. I'm feeling bad for her so I volunteer to go first. Shelley nods, looking grateful but wary.

"School," I say. "Having teachers who don't respect me. I guess that'd be the main thing." Actually, I think my self-esteem is fine. I have no doubt that I'm more intelligent than Mr. Lawson. But I have to say something, and Mr. Lawson's presence in my life is a definite problem.

Shelley smiles at me. "Good, Dante. Thanks. Parker? How about you?"

Parker shrugs. "Um, I feel okay, actually. But I guess maybe some old stuff. You know. My parents."

"Your parents," Shelley echoes encouragingly.

"I don't want to get into it."

I half expect Shelley to push her but she just nods. "Okay. That's fine. It's good that you're aware of it. Claire?"

"I think my own internal critic is a problem. My negative self-talk. I'm so hard on myself." Claire smiles widely like this is a good thing. "But I'm working on changing all those unhelpful messages into more affirming ones."

I catch Parker's eye and stifle a giggle.

"Jasmine?"

She shakes her head and whispers something. I didn't catch it, but Shelley thinks she did. "Being fat?" she asks. "Is that what you said?"

Jasmine flushes and shakes her head. "My dad, I said."

There's an awkward silence now that Shelley has basically called Jasmine fat. A nice way to end a session on self-esteem. Shelley's cheeks turn a mottled red, and oddly, for the first time, she seems like a real person to me. I feel almost as bad for her as I do for Jasmine.

Jasmine stares at the ground. Shelley obviously wants to move on and doesn't ask Jasmine more about her dad. "Marna?" she says.

The head-gear girl just makes a face and gestures at her orthodontia. Enough said.

"Nicki?"

Nicki runs her fingers through her short dark hair. "Coming here every Friday night," she says. "That'd be high on the list."

Shelley ignores her. I think she just wants to wrap it up and go home. "Sylvie? Your turn."

The redhead with the bandana. She's been pretty quiet all night, giving one-word answers. Now she looks up at Shelley, and I can see that she has tears streaking down her cheeks. "My mom," she whispers. "She's such a bitch. She hates me."

"Your mom…"

"We just had this huge fight after school because I asked if I could borrow the car to go see my boyfriend." She gives a hiccupping sob. "She's always calling me a slut and a whore…shit like that."

Christ. I can't imagine. The worst my mom ever does is try to persuade me to wear nail polish and take up scrapbooking.

Sylvie stays behind to talk to Shelley while the rest of us trickle out of the room. Parker catches my arm as we head up the stairs. "I'll call you, okay? To figure out when and where to pick you up?"

I nod. "Yeah. Call me."

Parker hops into her Civic and waves. I stand there, watching her leave.

Mom's full of questions when she picks me up, but I don't feel like talking about the group.

"It's all supposed to be confidential," I tell her. "You know. So people can talk about stuff that's private."

"But it was okay?"

"Yeah. I guess." I grin at her. "Don't worry so much, Mom."

"It's my job."

"And you're so good at it."

She laughs. "Well, kiddo. I'm afraid you're stuck with me."

"Yeah, yeah."

She sticks a CD in, and a country song starts to play. I lean back against the headrest, close my eyes and picture my phone number written on Parker's arm.

I hope she calls.

Mom drives me home; then she and Dad go out to a movie together. They've done this every Friday for as long as I can remember. It's funny—they're total opposites but they are still pretty lovey-dovey sometimes. I spend the evening surfing the Net and hoping Parker will call.

No messages from Beth. I can't believe I still bother checking. I look at the photograph of the two us, still in a frame on my dresser. In it, I'm laughing, but she's serious, concentrating on holding the camera too close to our faces. She's tanned and tall, pretty; nothing like Parker. God, I miss her.

I try to imagine what I'd talk to her about if she called. School, I guess, and how much I miss her. Blah blah blah. I couldn't tell her how I feel about Parker, even if I was clear about it myself. And when I think about describing the group at the church, I feel bad—it was so hokey but kind of sad too. I don't really want to make fun of anybody there, not even Shelley. And Beth would definitely not approve of what I'm planning to do Sunday night. She wouldn't see the point. It drove her crazy last year when I mouthed off in class. She was always asking me why. *Why do you do that, why create trouble for yourself, why make waves?* I didn't know why. I still don't know why.

I pick up the photo and drop it into my socks and underwear drawer, face down. *Good-bye, Beth.* Sometimes I almost hate her.

The phone rings and I jump on it. "Hello?"

"Hey."

"Parker?"

"Yeah, it's me. So…are you still in?"

"Course."

"Sunday night then. We'll pick you up."

"Yeah," I say. "No problem."

NINE

All weekend I can't stop thinking about Parker and her friends and what I've agreed to do. Half of me thinks I'm nuts, that I'll get caught and end up with a criminal record and be grounded for the rest of my life. The other half is just happy not to be thinking about Beth.

The plan is that Parker and her friends will pick me up at the corner of my street at eleven Sunday night. I'll wait until Mom and Dad are in bed; then I'll sneak out. I haven't done this before. I actually haven't lied to them much at all, but then again, I haven't had to. I've never been all that interested in partying, and my parents never objected to me going to Beth's. Hell, I could even sleep over there, and Mom just thought it was sweet that we were such good friends. I don't really want to lie to them now, but I can hardly tell them the truth about what I'm planning to do.

I feel pretty guilty about sneaking out, although not guilty enough to change my mind. Not as guilty as I probably should feel.

Dante Alighieri saved the ninth circle—the worst place of all, at the bottom of a great pit at the center of hell—for those who had betrayed people they were bound to, like their relatives. Okay, the examples in the poem are a bit more extreme than just lying to your parents one night, but still, his point was that betraying someone who trusts you is pretty much the worst thing you can do. That's as bad as it gets. The betrayers are forever imprisoned in Cocytus, which is basically a lake of ice frozen by the flapping of Satan's wings.

I shudder involuntarily. It's a good thing I'm not a believer.

Sunday night finally arrives. My parents stay up later than usual, and I start to get nervous. Ten o'clock. Only an hour until Parker and her friends will be at the corner of my street. I'm debating whether to go down and try to subtly remind them that it's bedtime when I hear Mom's footsteps on the stairs.

She knocks and opens my door almost simultaneously. "Hi, sweetie. Doing homework?"

"Mmm. Novel study." I hold up a book. "I'm doing *Tess of the D'Urbervilles.*"

"Didn't you already read that one?"

"Yeah."

"Oh. Well, great. That should be easy then."

"Uh-huh." And depressing. I'm already wishing I hadn't chosen this book.

"Well, I just wanted to say good night."

"Night, Mom," I say. "Sleep well." *Really, really well. And don't wake up until after I've snuck back in.*

"Love you."

"Love you too." I blow her a kiss and close the door behind her.

Mom and Dad are both snoring by ten thirty. I change into black jeans and a gray hoodie and stare at myself in the mirror. The buzzed hair makes my head look too small compared with the rest of me. When you're five foot eleven and broad-shouldered, you need hair. I bare my teeth at my reflection. There isn't much I can do about it other than wait for my hair to grow. I cram a navy hat over my fuzz, which helps a bit; then I brush my teeth and splash cold water on my face. Done.

I tiptoe down the carpeted stairs, pull on my jacket, lace my boots and slip out the front door with my heart racing.

Outside, the air is cool and damp. A heavy fog hangs low over the rooftops, and the streetlights are surrounded by fuzzy yellow halos. I jog to the street corner and wait there, checking my watch every few minutes. I hope no one looks out a window and sees me standing here. I can just imagine one of the neighbors reporting back to Mom. My hands are sweating and a small part of me hopes Parker and her friends won't show up. Then I hear a car, and a pair of headlights appears in the misty air. My heart speeds up, and I know there's no way I'm going to back out now.

"Dante!" A guy leans out the passenger window of a station wagon and gestures to me.

His head is half-shaved, leaving only a stripe of floppy dark hair a few inches wide. Like a Mohawk but not spiked up. I should fit right in with this crowd with my new do.

Someone opens the back door and I slide in.

Parker is sitting on the backseat beside me, her skinny face split by a huge grin.

"Hey, glad you could make it," she drawls.

"Hey," I say. "Good to see you again. I wasn't sure if you'd really show up."

"Are you kidding? This is a big occasion."

"What, stealing a sign?"

She shakes her head. "You. Our new member." The car pulls away from the curb, and Parker kicks the back of the driver seat. "Hey, assholes. How rude can you be? Aren't you guys going to introduce yourselves?"

"Maybe, if we could ever get a word in," the driver says.

His voice is slow and sort of smoky, both soft and rough at the same time. I look at him, curious, but all I can see from the backseat is long hair and one skinny shoulder.

"Ha ha. Very funny, Leo." Parker puts her arm around me. "Dante, meet Leo and Jamie. Guys, this is Dante."

Leo peers out the window and slows to a stop. He twists around to look at me. "Man, Dante. Nice to meet you. I thought I knew this area pretty well, but you live in a fucking maze, you know that? Look at this. Oak Place and Beech Crescent and Willow Terrace...What's that joke about the burbs? You know...where they..."

"Cut down the trees and name the streets after them," I say. "Yeah, yeah. I didn't choose to live here, okay?"

Floppy-Mohawk guy—Jamie—turns and looks at me too. "You choose to stay," he says.

"Like I have a choice," I say.

There is a long pause and everyone is very quiet. Apparently I just said the wrong thing. Jamie shrugs and turns away, as if he's already decided I'm not worth bothering with. Leo studies my face for a long moment, his eyes locked on mine. "You have more choices than you think," he says at last. All serious, like he's Yoda or something.

I don't say anything. My heart is beating so loud I think maybe everyone else can hear it too.

Finally Leo clears his throat. "Uh, Dante? Help me out here. How do I get back to the highway?"

I swallow and give him directions in a voice that sounds too fast and too uncertain. You know how some people end of all their sentences like they're asking a question? I hate that. But for some reason, that's what I'm doing.

Jamie turns on the radio; then he twists around in the passenger seat and grins at Parker and me. The mood in the car suddenly lightens. "So Parker talked you into coming along, hey?"

I shrug, pushing my thoughts aside. "She told me what you guys were planning and I said I'd help out."

"Uh-huh. You go to GRSS, right? What grade?"

"Eleven. You?"

He laughs. "Nah. I went to a school in the north end but I quit two years ago. The day I turned sixteen, I was out of there."

He's cute, despite the half-shaved hair thing, but not my type. Whatever that is. So far I've had precisely three relationships that could possibly be called romantic, and that's if you counted a week of note-passing and hand-holding with freckle-faced Mark Cole in the fifth grade. In grade nine, I went out briefly with a very intense grade-eleven guy called Lukas. He had these beautiful, long-lashed, dark eyes, and he wrote angst-filled poems for me and we talked on the phone until we fell asleep. Then he dumped me for no apparent reason, and I was both crushed and relieved.

And then there was Beth.

I watch the driveways flashing past outside and the yellow rectangles of illuminated house numbers glowing in the darkness: 3245, 3247, 3249, 3251. I sigh and turn my attention back to Jamie. "So, no regrets? About leaving school, I mean?"

"None."

"What do you do? You have a job?"

"Sure. Waiter at the Golden Griddle." He shrugs. "The tips are okay."

"That's how I met him," Parker says, bumping me with her shoulder as Leo takes a corner too fast. "I got a part-time job there last year, after school, and we started hanging out."

Jamie winks. "And the rest, as they say, is history."

"I left my parents' place a few weeks later." She makes a face. "It was about time."

I'd like to ask her about it, but this doesn't seem like the time or place. I remember what she said in the church basement, something about old stuff with her family and not wanting to get into it. A picture of that other girl's tear-streaked face slides into my mind. Sylvie, the redhead with the bandana. The girl whose mom called her a slut.

Leo turns onto the highway and steps on the gas. Parker lights a cigarette and holds it out her open window. The wind whips her pale hair straight back. "And then we met Leo at an anti-poverty demonstration and…"

"Started our little group," Jamie says, finishing her sentence. "Decided to do some stuff to fuck shit up."

Parker frowns at Jamie; then she turns and looks at me intently. "We never do anything without a good reason. I mean, we've talked a lot about what we believe and how we want to make some real changes in the world, you know? Right, Leo?"

Leo just nods.

I watch Parker's face as she talks and imagine the three of them sitting in coffee shops or driving around, talking late into the night. I've never known anyone I could have those kinds of conversations with. Mom's a big believer in not rocking the boat. And Dad—well, mostly he avoids talking. He doesn't spend much time with me, and when he does, he'd rather be doing other things at the same time. Raking leaves or painting his little soldiers. Besides, he hates conflict too much to disagree with Mom, let alone the government. Even Beth always thought that I should just accept things more and that trying to change things was pointless. *Quit banging your head against brick walls,* she used to say.

I don't think Parker believes in brick walls.

"What kind of changes?" I ask. I feel like I'm skating on the edge of something important and I want to keep this conversation going.

"Lots. Like, we think that everyone should be guaranteed a basic wage, you know? It shouldn't be that some people have practically nothing and other people have all the money."

Like my family, I think, wondering if they are all picturing our monster house and three-car garage. I clear my throat. "What else?"

She laughs. "I've got an opinion on most things. Don't get me started."

"I'm interested."

"Well, right now the school system is our main focus. But we support anti-poverty groups, animal rights groups, anti-war, social justice…I figure we all need to work together if we want to get anywhere."

Jamie twists around to face us. "Most of the groups

around here don't do anything. They just sit around and have endless meetings. They're all talk."

"Yeah, but you have to talk about things," Parker says. "You can't act without agreeing on some basic ideas first."

I can tell they've had this argument before.

"Most of those people are never going to do anything," Jamie says. "They talk and talk to avoid ever taking any action. That's why we started our own group. I got sick of all the fucking talk."

Leo's quiet, and I wonder what he is thinking. "My parents wouldn't let me do any of this," I say, thinking out loud. I brace myself, expecting Jamie to say something dismissive. But it's Parker who responds.

"So move out," she says.

I nod. "Maybe." I've always imagined I'd move out in two years, after grade twelve, to go to university. It's my parents' plan, not mine, but I've never questioned it before. I could move out, get a job, be done with school now. The thought is almost dizzying. I can't imagine being that free.

Then again, flipping pancakes at the Golden Griddle doesn't sound that much better than school.

The discussion spins off into talk about politics, government, social justice and most of all what Parker calls "compulsory education," which apparently just means making kids go to school. My head is spinning. I don't want to say too much because I haven't thought as much about all these issues as I should have, but at the same time, I am almost giddy with exhilaration. I'm sick of just reacting to things, putting up with things, waiting for things to change.

"Do you believe in fate?" I ask Parker, interrupting. "Like, that some things are inevitable? That you can't always alter what is going to happen?"

She looks at me like I'm nuts. "If you believed that, what would be the point in ever doing anything?"

"You're right," I say. "It'd be self-fulfilling, wouldn't it? You'd just give up and then you really wouldn't be able to control anything about your life."

She looks at me curiously but doesn't say anything.

I just grin at her. For the first time in ages, I actually feel like I could make things happen.

TEN

The whole area in front of the detention center is floodlit. There's even a light on the ground right in front of the sign, shining up through the sparse shrubbery.

I look at the others. "There's no way. If we make any noise at all, someone will look out and see us."

Jamie laughs, his lip curling in disgust. "I knew you'd wuss out."

"Don't be an asshole," Parker says quickly. She flicks her cigarette butt out the window and frowns. "You know, it is pretty bright."

"We've never been caught before," Jamie says. "We won't get caught this time either, unless we fuck it up."

I study the sign. It seems to be attached to the ground by two very thick wooden poles. More like tree stumps than poles, really. I can't imagine how we'd get it off, but I don't want to say anything else. I glance sideways at Parker and look away again, back out the window. The warm fizzy feeling I had in the car has disappeared and my stomach is in knots.

Jamie gets out of the car, and the rest of us follow. Parker looks pissed off, but she doesn't say anything, and I'm not sure if it's Jamie she's mad at or me. My heart is pounding so hard I feel like I've been running, and my hands are cold as ice. I don't think there is any way to do this without getting caught. I can just imagine my parents' reaction if they get a call from the cops. My mother will cry about a gallon of tears and demand to know what she's done wrong, Dad will be all silent and bewildered, and I'll be grounded for the rest of my life.

"Are you guys sure about this?" I ask. "I mean, I don't see how…"

Jamie ignores me. "We'll need the crow bar, Leo," he says. "Did you bring it?"

Leo nods. He shrugs off his leather jacket and tosses it on the driver's seat.

I realize he hasn't spoken a word since I first got in the car and he made that comment about choices. I look at him, curious despite my nervousness. He has surfer hair—brown streaked with blond, shoulder length—and a skinny face with dark eyes and a nice mouth. Not standard-cute the way Jamie is, but interesting-looking.

"Wait here a moment," he says. He's talking to all of us, but he's looking at Parker. She nods and grins at him like she's not worried about a thing. He walks over to the sign and inspects it closely. Then he looks at the building and the bright lights. "Get back in the car."

Just like that. All of us, even Jamie, do what he says. Leo starts the engine and quickly pulls out of the parking lot.

"What the hell, Leo?" Jamie turns to face him. "Did Dante get you spooked or something? We could've done it. We could've pried it off the posts and been gone before anyone knew anything was going on." He shoots me a dirty look. "I knew we shouldn't have let someone new join us."

"It's not Dante's fault," Parker protests.

Jamie is pissing me off. I want to hang out with Parker and her friends, but he's being totally irrational, and there's a limit to how much crap I'm prepared to take. I turn and glare at him. "You want to do it, go right ahead. I'm not stopping you."

Leo's voice cuts across our argument. "They had video cameras, okay? They'll have our license plate, our pictures...we're not doing this one."

"That sucks," Parker says. "It was such a great idea."

There is a long silence. Disappointment settles over us, so heavy and thick you can almost see it. When it comes down to it, I am actually kind of relieved about not having to steal anything, but it is hard to imagine simply going home now. And I have to admit I'd loved the idea of going to school tomorrow and seeing everyone's faces when they saw the sign. "Hey...," I say slowly.

"What?" Parker asks.

I find myself glancing over at Leo, but I can't see his face. "I was just thinking...well, what if we made a sign that said *Juvenile Detention Center*? And put it up at the school? Wouldn't that work almost as well?"

Jamie snorts. "What, like with paper and colored markers or something? That's lame."

My cheeks are hot, but I'm not going to let Jamie make me look like an idiot. "Whatever," I say. "Markers, paint, whatever. I mean, it's the message that's important, right?"

Parker nods excitedly. "I think it's a great idea. We could make it really big—like a banner, you know? And hang it right across the doors."

"It's not a bad idea," Leo says. He looks uneasily at Jamie; then he shrugs. "Let's do it."

"Jamie?" Parker's voice is soft. "Come on. It's better than nothing."

"Fine. Whatever." Jamie doesn't look at her.

Leo grins. "We'll go to your place then, okay? Do you have paper and stuff?"

"We could use a couple of white cotton sheets," Parker says. "We've got some old ones we used as drop sheets when we painted the apartment. Oh, and we've got left-over green paint too." She grins at me. "Dante, awesome idea. See, guys? I told you she rocked."

Leo laughs. Jamie doesn't say anything. An uneasy feeling shifts and settles in my stomach, but I ignore it.

Leo heads downtown and pulls up in front of a twenty-four-hour pizza joint. Jamie opens the door beside it, and we all troop up two flights of narrow stairs. At the top are two numbered doors. Jamie pulls a key out of his pocket and lets us into number four.

I look around the living room with its dark green walls and dirty gray carpet and feel a surge of excitement.

In the past, when I've gone to friends' places, their homes looked more or less like mine: parents hovering close by, offering us snacks; little brothers and sisters hanging around annoying us. I've never known anyone who had their own place.

"This is great," I say.

Parker laughs. "It's a dive. But at least my parents don't live here." A shadow flickers behind her eyes. "At least I don't have to take orders from them or listen to them fighting all night."

I don't know what to say.

"Sheets." Jamie dumps a pile of white cloth on the floor. "I'll get the paint."

Parker follows Jamie. Leo kneels on the floor and starts spreading out the sheets. "I'm glad you've joined our group," he says. He sits back on his heels and looks at me for a long time.

I start to squirm under his gaze. I clear my throat and grab the other end of the sheet to help straighten it out and to give me an excuse to look away. "Sure," I say. "Me too."

"Do I make you uncomfortable?"

"No. It's fine. I'm fine."

"Sorry. I do, don't I? Parker says I make too much eye contact."

I look up at him, surprised. "She does?"

"Yeah. She says I freak people out. That I'm too intense."

"I don't think you're too intense."

"Me neither. I think most people aren't intense enough."

I laugh.

He laughs too; then he shakes his head. "I mean it. Most people are like...diluted. Anaesthetized, you know? They go around all numbed out by TV or religion or trash media, brainwashed, not thinking for themselves."

"My mother's like that," I blurt. "She's all about scrapbooking and keeping our house looking like a show home and making sure her nails are perfectly manicured. Like that's what she thinks is important in life." I feel a twinge of guilt. I know I'm not being fair to my mom. *Appearances are what people judge us by*, she says. *It may not be fair but that's the way it is.*

"Exactly." Leo holds my gaze again. "People don't really connect with each other. They're all in their own little bubbles."

"Yes. Yes!" The words tumble out. "That's just how it is." I think about how I move through my days at school, feeling so alone half the time even though I'm surrounded by people. "Like we're all on separate islands and we don't ever meet up at all. We just sort of...float on by." I've mixed up his bubble metaphor with my island one, but he doesn't seem to notice.

Leo starts to roll a joint. "Smoke?"

"No. I don't do drugs."

"It's totally natural, you know? And it's way less addictive than alcohol. Shouldn't be illegal."

I shake my head. "You don't have to convince me. I don't have a problem with it or anything; I just don't like how it makes me feel."

"How's that?"

I think about the handful of times I've tried it with the stoners at school. "Um, sort of anxious, I guess."

"Probably bad stuff. Not pure, you know?"

People who smoke pot always want you to join them. Like Linnea and her friends at school. I don't get it. I'd be happy to hang out with them and not smoke, but it's like they take it personally or something. Like I'm criticizing them. I get tired of explaining that I'm just not into it. "I'm a runner," I say instead. "I like to keep my lungs clean."

"Hey, slackers." Jamie puts down two large paint cans, long ribbons of dried paint caked on their sides. Parker steps into the room behind him and looks at Leo and then at me. Her arms are full of assorted paintbrushes.

"Well," Jamie says. "Let's get to work."

ELEVEN

It is two in the morning when we finish the sign.

"I'd better get home," I say reluctantly. The room is smoky and my eyes are stinging. "My mom gets up at six."

Parker stands up and stretches. "I'll drive you."

Leo folds up the sign, careful not to smudge the still tacky paint. "How about Dante and I go? We can hang the sign, and then I'll run her home."

"Cheers," Jamie says. "Parker and I should hit the sack. We both have to work in the morning." He yawns. "Flipping pancakes."

It is weird driving through the empty streets with Leo, and even weirder pulling up to GRSS in the middle of the night. Dark, quiet and oddly unfamiliar.

"So this is where you spend your days," Leo says.

I nod. "This is it."

"And?"

"It's boring. Really boring." I can't quite meet his eyes. Parker's right: He makes too much eye contact. There's something about the way he holds my gaze that makes it hard to breathe. "Where did you go to school?" I ask, pushing my feet against the floor of the car.

There's a long silence. Finally Leo nods out the window. "Right here," he says.

"Here? You did? When?"

His hands are white-knuckled around the steering wheel. "Quit two years ago," he says. "I did grade nine and ten here, quit part way through grade eleven."

I do the math. "So you must have left right before I started."

"I guess so." He shakes his head slowly. "I hated it."

I remember his comments about the suburbs. I guess he hates it not because he's an outsider but because he knows it all too well. I glance at my watch: two thirty. I know we should get moving and hang the sign, but I don't want to stop talking. "Did you ever have Mr. Lawson?"

"Nazi," he says. "Power-tripping Nazi. I hated him."

I have a bit of a problem with people using the word *Nazi* like that—I mean, much as I hate Lawson, there isn't really any comparison. Usually I say something, but this time I let it slide. "Me too. You know, he pretty much accused me of lying when I said I'd already read the assigned books."

"He grabbed me by the collar once and shoved me up against the lockers."

"Jesus. Can teachers do that? I mean, that's...isn't that assault?"

He gives me a shark-like grin. "You'd think. But it was his word against mine. You can guess who the principal believed."

"Jesus," I say again. "That's awful." I think back to my conversation with Mrs. Greenway. "The new principal is okay. I think she believes me. I don't think she even likes Mr. Lawson."

"Sure." Leo stares out the front window at the school. "But when it really matters, wait and see whose side she takes. They're all the same."

I pull my lower lip between my teeth. I've always liked Mrs. G., but it isn't like she's actually taken my side in any way that counts. She hasn't challenged Lawson or let me transfer out of his class. So I don't know. Maybe Leo is right.

He opens his door. "I guess we'd better hang the sign, hey?"

We get out of the car and dump the bundle of sheets on the ground.

"We should hang it so it completely covers the front doors," Leo says.

I shake my head. "No. The teachers get in early—they'll just take it down." I look at the school building thoughtfully. "I think we should hang it high. Really high."

Leo follows my gaze and frowns. The building is two stories high, a sheer gray cliff. "How?" he asks. "We can't climb up there."

I study the building and don't answer for a minute. A concrete awning juts out over the doors, and above it the wall stretches straight up to join a sloping shingle roof. It's crazy, but I'm overcome with a reckless desire to impress him. "I think we could do it," I say. "The first part would be hardest. Once we're on top of the awning, it's just a couple of feet over to one side to reach that window. Then from the window frame to the roof…"

"Uh, Dante? That wall is vertical." He looks a bit embarrassed. "Jamie could probably do it, but I'm not so good with heights."

I laugh. "I'm nearly six feet tall. I'm used to heights." I study the building. Not totally easy, but possible. I've done some climbing with my Dad and I'm not bad at it. Of course, I've never actually climbed a building before. Climbing buildings wasn't really in Dad's repertoire.

"This is crazy," he says. "If we slipped, we'd be dead."

I just shrug. "I never slip." I look up at the wall again. He's right. Slipping would be a very bad idea. Then I look back at Leo. "I guess I'm on my own."

Five minutes later, I'm climbing. I feel like a spider—all skinny arms and legs clinging to the gray bricks. It's physical and it's mental, but it's nothing like running. It's slow, almost agonizingly slow, and instead of pushing myself to go faster, I'm forcing myself to wait, to pause, to think. Instead of switching my brain off, I feel like every neuron is firing at once. Like my brain is in survival mode and my body is pulsing with adrenaline. If I survive this, I'll be high for a week.

It's a cold night, clear and starry, and there'll be frost in the morning. My fingers ache with both chill and strain, and sweat trickles down my face and stings my eyes. I make it onto the awning and rest for a moment, eyeing the second floor window just off to one side. It's set in a wide concrete frame that sticks out a couple of inches from the bricks. Good enough.

I reach over with one hand and then the other, gripping the top edge with my fingertips. I'm pretty sure I can make it. I hold my breath, stretching...

And my foot slips.

For a split second, I am hanging from my fingers. I can hear my heart beating. I close my eyes and feel around with my foot. There. I pull both feet up to the window ledge and pause for a moment to catch my breath.

"God," I whisper under my breath. Like I said, I'm an atheist, but it almost feels like a thank-you just the same.

"Thought you never slipped," Leo says hoarsely. He's trying to sound casual, but I figure I've probably just about given him a heart attack.

"Shhh," I say. "No problem. I'm almost there." It occurs to me that none of Dante's circles of hell involved heights. He's got all kinds of other punishments: high winds, stinging insects, ice, fire, even having your head fixed on backward for eternity—but no heights. I'd think having to spend forever balanced on a narrow ledge would be pretty nasty. Though if you're already dead, maybe falling isn't so bad.

I can't believe I'm doing this without ropes or anything.

I'm about to move when I hear sirens. I freeze, my body pressed tight to the window. Cops. Out of the corner of my eye, I can see the flash of red and blue lights. My breathing is fast and shallow and my arms are aching. What the hell am I doing here? It suddenly seems stupid and suicidal; this whole night seems unreal.

The cop cars come closer. I hold my breath.

Then the lights are gone, past us, and the sirens grow fainter. I glance down to see that Leo has hit the dirt.

"Jesus Christ. Hurry up, Dante," he whispers, scrambling back to his feet.

"You want to try it?" I hiss back. "See how fast you can climb?"

He shakes his head. "No. Sorry." He steps closer to the school. "Cops just freak me out. Don't listen to me. Don't rush."

"Yeah." I blink sweat from my eyes. Time to get off this wall.

The last part is tricky. I manage to pull myself up so that I am standing on the top edge of the concrete around the window frame. Just above me, the roof has a slight overhang and I have to lean back slightly to grab the edge. When you're standing on a tiny concrete sill two stories up, leaning backward is not appealing. I don't like this at all. I know I can do it—I've done it before on a rock face—but I still have to force myself, mind over muscle.

From the ground, I could see a metal pipe running down the roof, but now I can't see anything but the smooth gray bricks right in front of my face. I force myself to breathe slow and easy and move an inch at a time, sideways, feeling along the edge. Finally my fingertips bump cold metal. I give the pipe a gentle tug, then a harder one. Secure.

I take a breath. Then I heave myself up as hard as I can. I don't quite make it up all the way, but I get one leg up and manage to hook my foot and knee over the edge. Then I haul myself up the rest of the way and crawl a couple of feet away from the edge. I sit on the sloping roof, heart pounding.

"Christ." Leo's voice cracks. "I never want to see anyone do anything like that again." He sinks slowly to the ground. "I think I might throw up."

I laugh, feeling the adrenaline rushing through me like a tide. I can't believe I've done it. "Okay," I yell back, grinning. "When you're done puking, I'll pull up the sign."

Leo tosses up the rope. It takes three attempts, but finally I catch it. I pull on the rope, and slowly the bundle of sheets slides and jerks its way up to me. Piece of cake. I unfold it: three sheets stapled together with a hammer and nails wrapped inside it. The sign looks just as big up on the roof as it did stretched out in Parker and Jamie's apartment.

I hammer nails in two corners to secure it to the roof; then I let it drop.

When I am safely on the ground, I finally let myself look back up at the school. The sign looks amazing way up there. There is no way anyone arriving at the school can miss it. Huge green letters read *JUVENILE DETENTION CENTER*.

Leo puts one arm over my shoulders. "You're okay, Dante."

"We make a good team," I say. Then I blush. I hope he doesn't read anything into that. "I mean, you know…"

His eyes are dark and intense. "Dante?"

"Yeah?" My voice comes out sounding funny.

"Parker was right. You rock." Leo pulls me close. Then he kisses me.

For a second, I kiss him back. Maybe it'll be different this time, I think. But it isn't. It's okay; it's fine. I don't hate kissing him or anything. It's just not me. It's not what I want. I pull away. "Look, I don't know…"

He lets me go. "Sorry. I just…I shouldn't have done that."

"Yeah." My legs are trembling but it's from the climb, not the kiss. "It's okay." I look at him. He is actually taller than me, which most guys are not. Behind him, I can see a faint lightness on the horizon. It's almost five o'clock. "I better get home," I say. "I have to pretend to be asleep for an hour, until my parents get up."

Leo laughs, but it sounds harsh and discordant, like he's not really amused, like nothing's really funny at all.

"Yeah," he says. "From one fucking jail to another. That's life for you."

We're both quiet in the car. Leo smokes a cigarette, and I play with the radio dial, trying to find decent music. Occasionally one of us says something like *Wow, that was amazing,* or *I can't believe we did that.* When Leo drops me off, neither of us mention the kiss—we just say good-bye like nothing happened.

I manage to sneak back into the house without waking my parents, but there is no way I can sleep. I lie in bed and watch the cracks around my blinds grow slowly brighter and wonder when I'll see Leo or Parker again. My heart is still pounding, my muscles twitching, all systems on alert. I'm not usually a big risk-taker. I wear a seat belt, I don't do drugs, you couldn't pay me to go bungee jumping. Climbing that school was the stupidest, craziest, riskiest thing I've ever done.

I feel like this should concern me, but for some reason it doesn't.

I have just started to doze when my alarm goes off. My whole body jerks like crazy and for a second I think I'm falling. My arms flail about, and then I'm fully awake. I sit up, gasping. I guess my body still thinks I'm on that wall.

Or maybe it's more than that. Maybe it's the way everything I've always taken for granted—school, my family, future plans, my whole life—suddenly seems like it isn't as solidly built as I'd thought. It's a big precarious pile, teetering wildly, and I'm balanced on top. I feel like it all might come crashing down. I feel like everything is about to change.

I rub my hands over my face and get out of bed. The muscles in my shoulders are sore, my arms heavy, my hands scratched up. I pull on jeans and a few layers of baggy shirts, debate the hat and decide to let my fuzz go free. Then I make my way downstairs.

"How are you feeling?" Mom asks. "Good sleep?"

"Yeah." Thanks for the prompt, Mom. "Good sleep."

She is standing at the counter drinking decaf, wearing a pink silk housecoat. "You want toast, right?"

"Right. Thanks."

She sticks a piece of bread in the toaster for me and hands me a glass of orange juice. "There you go, Emily."

I sigh. "Dante. Not Emily."

"Sorry, honey."

She calls me honey a lot. I figure it's easier for her than having to say Dante. I take a sip of the juice and look around the sunny kitchen with its dark wood and granite countertops and brand-new stainless-steel appliances; I think about sitting on the dirty carpet at Parker and Jamie's place, painting green letters on white sheets.

It feels like it could all have been some crazy dream.

Mom eyes me and shakes her head. "That haircut. And you had such lovely hair too."

"Drop it, already," I say. My voice is sharper than I mean it to be. It's just that from the way Mom has gone on about it, you'd think that haircuts actually mattered. You'd think haircuts rated alongside global warming and third-world debt in the scale of what is important.

She looks a bit taken aback but says nothing. I spread peanut butter and jam on my toast and try to imagine what it would be like to live on my own. The idea is weirdly disorienting.

I'm sixteen. I could do it. I even have enough money in the bank for a few months' rent. It's supposed to be for later, for college, but...

"You're awfully quiet," Mom says. "Everything okay?"

Dad glances up from behind the paper.

I nod. It is so weird that I was out all night and they don't know. I'm not remotely worried about them guessing. Even if I told them, I'm pretty sure they wouldn't believe me.

TWELVE

I walk back to the school at eight thirty. I've been gone less than four hours, but it feels like a different place in the daylight. There is a crowd gathered outside, twenty or thirty kids, all staring up at the sign on the roof.

"I don't get it," one girl says. She's in grade twelve; I recognize her but don't know her name. A cheerleader. *"Juvenile Detention Center?"*

Another girl frowns. "Me either."

I want to say something, but I bite my lip and stare at the sign like everyone else.

Three girls from my homeroom class are standing near me. Jackie and Nicole and Linnea. They turn to me, three pairs of heavily outlined eyes open wide. Linnea grins at me. "Did you see this?"

I nod. "Hey. Uh, yeah, it'd be kind of hard to miss." I wonder what she'd say if I told her I hung it up there. Probably she'd think I was joking.

"Can you believe this?" Nicole demands. She looks like she hasn't washed her hair all weekend. It hangs across her face, straight as uncooked spaghetti.

Jackie folds her arms across her chest and looks up at the sign. "Are they slagging GRSS? It's stupid. This is an awesome school."

Go figure. Even the stoners like it here. So what is wrong with me?

Nicole laughs. "I wonder how the hell they got the sign up on the roof."

I can't believe they don't get it. That they're not even talking about what matters. They are all missing the point. "Well…," I start slowly, "I think it's kind of interesting. I mean, if you think about it, there are some similarities between school and prison."

They both stare at me blankly.

"Look at Mr. Lawson," I say. "He'd make a great prison guard."

Nicole laughs again. "Yeah. He's a tool."

The bell rings. Some students start to drift in but not me.

"And look at all the rules," I say. "A bell rings, so everyone goes inside. And we have to be here, whether we want to or not."

"Well, we don't *really* have to," Linnea points out.

A voice behind us cuts across the conversation. "All right folks, let's move it." It's a teacher. "Excitement's over. Get to class."

Everyone scurries through the doors. I hesitate for a second, remembering Leo's words: *You have more choices than you think.* It's true. I could turn around and walk away. But instead I push through the doors, walk down the hall and sit down in Mr. Lawson's stupid English class.

Even before class begins, people have stopped talking about the sign. Other than a few comments about who might have done it, no one seems to care. I don't know exactly what I hoped for, but more than this anyway.

By morning break, the sign is gone. And by lunchtime, everyone seems to have forgotten about it.

Except me.

After school, I head upstairs to check my e-mail. Nothing from Beth, of course, or anyone else for that matter. I wish I could send Parker a message, but I don't have her e-mail address. Actually, I don't know if she even has a computer. Probably not.

I hope Leo didn't tell her about the kiss. I'm not sure why exactly, but I don't want her to know. It's not that I think she'd mind. I suspect she might actually be pleased about it—her and Jamie, me and Leo. I guess it would have a certain symmetry. Two neat little equations. Something about it makes me feel squirmy. I don't want Parker to be pleased. I want her to mind.

I find myself thinking about Beth, and how we ended up together without ever talking about it or even seeing it coming. It just happened one day after we'd been hanging out for a few weeks. We'd gone for a run together after school and then gone back to her place.

I chew my lip, remembering. We were up in her room, laughing and goofing around, and Beth had been putting makeup on me, which was kind of funny because I didn't usually wear any. She put thick eyeliner on me and told me I looked like Amy Winehouse.

"I do not," I said, giving her a shove. She fell onto her bed, laughing.

"But much cuter," she said.

I poked her in the ribs. "Amy Winehouse. As if. She's scary. Take it back."

She grabbed me. "You do, you do. It's your eyes, Emily. It's the whole 'nobody knows my pain' emo thing."

I sat on her, straddling her hips, holding her arms above her head. "Take it back, Beth, or I'll tickle you. No mercy." She wriggled an arm free and pulled me down on the bed, tickling my ribs, and we were rolling around, wrestling, cracking up.

Then somehow it changed, just like that. We weren't laughing anymore. We were staring at each other, our faces inches apart, and there were maybe two seconds where either one of us could have made a joke or pulled away, but neither of us did. Then we were kissing, and it was so intense I could barely breathe, and then we were touching each other and we'd crossed that line, we were miles over that line, and there was no going back. It felt like we'd been waiting for this but without knowing it.

Remembering it still makes my heart race.

In that instant we'd slipped from being friends into something more. But we never talked about it, never named it, never acknowledged it in any way. We never admitted we were anything but best friends. Running buddies.

I look at my dresser and see the empty space. I'd forgotten that I'd put the picture of Beth away in my drawer. Good-bye Beth. I wish it were that easy. I wish I could just forget about her. A line from *Inferno* slips into my mind: *The double-grief of a lost bliss is to recall its happy hour in pain.* I underlined it as soon as I read it, even though I hardly ever write in my books. It is just so true.

I check Facebook and find that Beth has changed her picture. The one I took is gone and the new one she's put up doesn't even look like her. Her hair is blonder and cut to shoulder-length, and she's looking off to one side, distracted, smiling. A couple of guys are standing behind her, holding drinks—it's a party picture.

My throat feels like I've swallowed a knife, but I can't seem to cry. I've never been a good crier; I just get all tight and choked up and can't talk. *Goddamn it, Beth.* Everything that happened between us seemed so easy and natural when she was here, but it all hangs over me now, an unspoken, painful, confusing mess.

Then I notice that she's updated her profile. It now reads: *Beth is in love.*

Obviously she doesn't mean with me.

It's okay, I guess. I'm not in love with her either. Not really, not anymore. Still, I can't help wishing she could have told me herself. I wonder who she's met. A guy, obviously, or she wouldn't be talking about it on Facebook.

She sure didn't talk about us on Facebook. Not that I wanted her to. I mean, it's the twenty-first century, but people are still assholes about some things. Besides, I kind of liked the fact that our parents had no issues with us having sleepovers. Mom would've flipped if she knew.

Still, I'd have liked to at least know we were a couple, in Beth's mind as well as mine. But I wasn't ever sure. Beth wouldn't even talk about us when we were alone together. I tried a couple of times, and she basically told me that if I didn't drop it, it would all be over. She started crying, getting all shaky and freaked out. *I can't deal with this, Emily. I don't want to talk about it.*

I did, desperately. I wanted to talk about everything. I wanted to talk about what it all meant, about me and about us. I wanted to tell her how I felt about her, and to know if she felt the same way about me. But I didn't want to lose her, and I didn't want to go back to just being friends. So I dropped it.

I look at her picture on the screen for a few seconds longer, wondering if one of those guys in the photo is the one she's in love with. Then I close my laptop.

I think about Parker, and then about Leo and that kiss. I close my eyes. It'd be so much easier to go out with a guy, so much less complicated. And I like Leo. I do.

But it's Parker I can't stop thinking about.

I don't see Parker all week. I keep hoping she'll show up with another stack of crazy flyers. I pass the time in class by doodling new slogans for her. *Stop brainwashing kids. GRSS: Enforcing Conformity. Schools are Factories—Get off the Assembly Line.* And my personal fave: *GRSS: the Tenth Circle.* I love it, but no one else would get it.

By Friday, I find myself in the bizarre situation of almost looking forward to Social Skills 101. At least Parker will be there. I wonder if she and Leo and Jamie are planning anything else.

"You've got your group tonight," Mom reminds me after school. Her eyes are on my face, sharply focused, as if she's watching for signs of resistance. I can see her getting primed to point out that I'd agreed to go to at least two sessions before making up my mind.

"I know," I say, injecting a note of weariness into my voice. I don't want her to think I'm too keen, or god knows what else she'll sign me up for. "I haven't forgotten."

"Good, good. I'm sure you'll make some new friends there. I have such a good feeling about it." She smiles at me. "Someone to take Beth's place maybe."

An image of Parker's face slides into my head. *Someone to take Beth's place.* My cheeks are warm. If Mom knew what she was saying..."Yeah, maybe," I say; then I change the subject. "Did you get your teeth whitened or something?"

She covers her mouth with her hand and laughs.

"You did!"

Dad looks up from his food, which has been occupying his full attention. He has these weird eating habits. He cuts everything into little squares—tiny cubes of chicken, potato, zucchini. Stuff like rice that can't be cut up gets arranged into little piles. Mountain ranges, or miniature pyramids. If we have company, he eats like a normal person, but when it's just us, he won't take a bite until his plate looks like some bizarre food mosaic.

"Laser-whitening," Mom says. She drops her hand and bares her bleached teeth at us. "They were getting yellow. Sort of horsey-looking, you know?"

"Looked fine to me," Dad says and returns his attention to his plate.

"Honestly, sometimes I don't know why I bother." Mom gives a little sigh and turns to me. "Emily, you should get yours done too. They're pretty white anyway, but there's always room for improvement."

Dad's eyes flick back up for a second and catch mine. Sometimes I think we can read each other's minds. *NFW*, that's what I'm thinking. No fucking way. He gives me a tiny grin but says nothing. If Mom makes an appointment at the dentist for him, he won't argue. He'll just forget to go.

What kind of bird is it that ends up hatching the cuckoo's eggs? That's Mom, anyway. I'm her cuckoo child. She finds me utterly bewildering but she does her best to take care of me anyway.

After dinner I change into my favorite, soft, faded jeans and pull a black V-neck sweater over my white T-shirt. I debate whether to wear a baseball cap but decide against it. Instead I use a bit of Dad's extra-strength hair gel and run my fingers through my hair until it's spiky and messed up. Mom will hate this, but it actually looks pretty good.

The adrenaline from last Sunday's climb wore off days ago, but it's left me feeling restless and sort of hungry. I want something to happen. I open my bedroom window. At our old house, I could lean right out, but these ones only slide a few inches. Safety windows. I push my nose against the screen. It's getting dark and the driveway lights are all on, two glowing spheres at the end of every driveway, like radioactive bowling balls. A pair for each nuclear family, marking off the edges of the wide road. A 747 could land on Willow Terrace, no problem.

I slam the window closed, harder than I mean to, and head downstairs.

Parker isn't at the church when I arrive. I'm a few minutes early: Mom's a big believer in punctuality.

The circle of chairs is set up in the middle of the room, empty except for Shelley. I don't want to sit there waiting under the fluorescent lights, so I loiter by the doorway reading the Jesus posters. *Interested in Converting to*

Catholicism? one asks. *Join our class, Tuesday evenings, open to all.* Another has a candle and the words *You Are the Light of the World.*

Shelley clears her throat. I turn around and smile at her with this involuntary grin I get when I'm uncomfortable.

"Welcome back, Dante. I'm so glad you're here." She pats the seat beside her.

At least she got my name right. I walk across the room and sit down, crossing my ankle over my knee and wishing I'd brought a book to read, or pretend to read, until the others arrive. Shelley is way too enthusiastic, I decide. It's not that she's phony—that would almost be easier—it's that she's depressingly, embarrassingly, sincere. I wonder what the rest of her life is like, if she has a boyfriend or a full-time job, whether she lives alone, why she does this kind of work. I wonder if she has any friends and what she tells them about us and about this group. It's weird to think about.

The others all drift in, one by one, and I try to remember their names. Sylvie, the redhead who cried. Nicki, the dark-haired mouthy one. The silent girl with braces, whose name I have forgotten again. The annoying Shelley wannabe, Claire. Jasmine.

But no Parker.

She has my phone number, I think, remembering how I wrote it on her arm last week under the pale lights in the parking lot. She could have called me if she wasn't coming.

"Well," Shelley says, beaming a hundred-watt smile at us all. "It is six-oh-five. That is past our start time. Let's begin."

She lifts her fingers and makes these scratchy quote marks in the air when she says "start time." *Start time.* I feel a flash of anger toward her, as if by starting the group she's closing off the possibility that Parker might still show up.

"We'll start with check-in," she says. "I'd like to hear how you are all feeling this week, so let's see…" She taps her lower lip with her fingertip. "Tell me, if you were a weather system, what would you be and why?"

My heart sinks. If Parker were here, if I could exchange glances with her across the circle, this might be bearable. But without her…"Uh, Shelley? Can I just run to the bathroom? I mean, go ahead and start…"

She nods and sighs. "We'll wait."

"No, no. Don't wait. Just go ahead with, you know, the weather thing."

Shelley purses her lips for a moment before speaking. "Dante. Opening check-in is an important part of our *group process*. It helps us all bring our full selves here, to this moment, fully present and connected to each other."

More scratchy quote marks for *group process*. I remember my conversation with Leo about how people don't really connect. I don't want to be fully present. I don't even want to be partially present.

Shelley smiles and her eyes flick from one girl to the next as if she can forge connections by the sheer power of her gaze. "We'll wait for you."

I don't think genuine connection is something you can force like this, but I stand up and walk away from the circle without saying anything.

In the washroom, a framed pink poster reads *Have you made God smile today?* I splash cold water on my face and contemplate making a run for it, even though I know I won't really do it. No one is preventing me from walking out the door, but it still doesn't really feel possible.

The bathroom mirror is flecked with splashes of dried soap and gunk. I stare at my reflection. My eyes are bloodshot, and under the fluorescent lights, my skin has a weird grayish tinge. I head back to the circle, feeling trapped and miserable.

The door opens and Parker walks in. My heart leaps, and I can't help the huge grin that spreads across my face. It's like the lights in the room suddenly got brighter. Like the sun came out from behind a cloud.

"Sorry I'm late," she says cheerfully. "Did I miss much?"

"Not at all." Shelley claps her hands together like a little kid. "We're just about to begin."

Parker drops into the seat beside me and bends close. "Nice going, Spider Girl," she whispers.

I'm still grinning as Claire begins to explain exactly how and why she feels like a spring shower.

THIRTEEN

At break, Parker and I head outside so she can have a smoke. It's dark and a cold rain is falling, puddles shining around the scattering of cars in the small parking lot. We stand by the doors, pushing our backs against the wall of the church and trying to shelter under the overhanging roof. Parker lights her cigarette, and a fat raindrop splats against my cheek.

"So what happened at your school?" she asks. "Sorry I never called." She gestures at her arm. "I took a shower and then I realized I never wrote your number down anywhere else. All I could read was a three and an eight. Anyway, did the sign get people talking?"

I shake my head. "Not so much. Everyone is so wrapped up in their own little lives that they hardly seemed to notice. I swear, it'd take a bomb going off to get their attention."

"We've talked about that," Parker says. "It's not as easy as you'd think."

"Jesus, Parker. I was kidding."

She laughs. "Well, sure. Me too. You didn't think I was serious?"

I swallow. "No. Of course not." Actually, for a second I'd wondered. There's something about Jamie that I don't quite trust. I don't know how far he'd go. "So, are you planning anything else?"

"Are you in?" I nod, and she grins at me. "Leo said you would be."

"He did?"

"Yeah." She looks at me like she might say something more, but then she just shakes her head.

My heart quickens. I wonder if he told her about the kiss. "Um, Parker?"

"What?"

"I don't know. Nothing." Another raindrop splats on the top of my head and trickles down my forehead. I wipe it away with the back of my hand. "What are you planning? Another sign or something? Or more flyers?"

"I don't know. Leo's been going on about your school, wanting to do something else there." She gives me a sideways look. "He went to GRSS, you know."

"Yeah. So he said."

"He's never said much about school before. Not about his own experience, I mean." Parker looks at me like she's waiting for me to fill in some blanks, but I doubt I know anything she doesn't.

"He didn't say much to me. Only that he had the same asshole teacher that I have now."

"He quit two years ago. I was kind of surprised at how intense he still is about it." She flicks her cigarette butt into a puddle. "And he's told Jamie, and now…well, you can imagine. Jamie's not so much into talking, but he's got a real hate on for your school. It's his new obsession. He's all, like, let's do something already."

"Like what?"

She shrugs. "I don't know. Why don't you come round sometime? We can hang out. Plan something, maybe."

Mom won't like the idea of me hanging out with someone who has her own place. She'll assume that Parker is trouble, just because she doesn't live at home. "Okay," I say. I don't want to miss out on anything, and I want to see Parker again. So I guess I'll just have to figure out how to swing it.

The doors open beside us, and Shelley sticks her head out, tapping her watch. Parker and I follow her down the stairs and back into the group room, where Shelley has been busy. A giant sheet of paper is spread over a long table. Little pots of glue are carefully placed every couple of feet, and markers, scissors and pastels are laid out at one end. At the other end is a cardboard box filled with pictures cut from magazines. I pick up a picture of a running shoe and turn it over in my hand.

"We're going to make a group mural," Shelley announces.

"Oh! Or maybe we could do a 'zine," Nicki says. "As a group, you know?" Her voice sounds different than usual, and I realize I've never heard her sound remotely enthusiastic about anything before.

Shelley shakes her head. "Not a 'zine. A mural. Something that represents our shared struggles and our combined strength."

Nicki ignores her. "Sylvie's poems, Jasmine's artwork, Parker's weird conspiracy theories, my...I don't know. I'll write something. We could all write stuff. It could be called, um..."

"Of course I'm in favor of young women finding their voices..." Shelley sticks the capped end of a marker in her mouth and sucks on it thoughtfully; then she shakes her head. "But I wouldn't want some...project...to distract from the therapeutic focus of this group."

Parker sighs audibly and rolls her eyes. "It'd be good for our self-esteem, Shelley," she says, straight-faced. "It'd be empowering."

I start to laugh. "Yes, Shelley. It'd be so *empowering*."

"Well." Shelley looks around like she's suspects she's being made fun of. "I'll think about it, okay? But for now...a group mural. Painting. Collage."

"I am so not into art," Nicki says sullenly.

"At least we don't have to talk," I whisper to Parker.

She rolls her eyes. "Want to bet?"

Shelley smiles at Nicki as if she hasn't just totally squashed her creativity. "So not into art," she echoes, looking meaningfully from one of us to the next as if she is distributing Nicki's words around the group. "Does anyone else share Nicki's feelings? Let's hear from each of you."

Parker calls me later that night. A lot later. I run for the phone, toothbrush in hand.

Dad steps into the hallway, frowning, and shakes his head at me.

"Can you come round tomorrow?"

I think for a moment. Saturday. "What time?"

"Leo says he could pick you up after dinner. We're going to meet at my place."

My parents aren't going to be too thrilled with the idea of some skinny, long-haired, older guy picking me up in his beater station wagon. "Umm, I don't know."

"Come on. You said your mom made you go to that group tonight because she wants you to make friends." She laughs. "So tell her you made some friends."

"Maybe." I bite my lip, thinking. "Okay. But tell Leo he doesn't have to pick me up. I'll figure out a way to get there."

I spend half the night strategizing and finally decide to take Parker's advice. At breakfast, I tell Mom that I'm going to meet a friend at the mall to catch a movie. A new friend.

"Really? A new friend?" Her eyes are thoughtful.

"From the group," I say. "You know, the social skills group?"

"Well." She stares at me. I think she is torn between her suspicions that it is too good to be true and her hopes that I might not be a complete loner forever. "That's wonderful."

"Yeah, I guess you were right." I know this is overkill, but I can't seem to stop. I'm not a good liar. When I'm nervous, I talk too much.

"What movie are you going to see?"

I have no idea what's playing. "Um, some comedy."

"And your new friend...a girl?"

I nod.

"What's her name?"

At least I can answer one question honestly. "Parker."

"Parker. That's unusual." She sips her coffee, still watching me, her face serious. "Emily..."

I tense. "What?"

"Would you like me to try to get an appointment for you with my hairdresser? It's short notice, but maybe she could squeeze you in this afternoon. So you'd look nice for tonight."

I blow out a short breath of relief. "It's not a date, Mom."

"Well, obviously not." She looks horrified, or maybe just startled. Apparently that possibility hasn't occurred to her yet. "But still. If you're going out..."

"No thanks. I think it'd be better to let it grow some more first."

"Well, you might be right," she concedes, studying my hair thoughtfully.

Enough about my hair. "So, do you think I could get a ride to the mall after dinner? The one downtown?"

"Of course, honey. No problem." She smiles at me. "I'm so glad the group has worked out so well. I had such a good feeling about it."

"Thanks," I say. I try not to feel guilty.

I go for a long run; then I spend the rest of the day re-reading *Tess of the D'Urbervilles* and making notes. I'm finding the book infuriating this time around. I want Tess to forget about the guy she's so hung up on and get herself a life. Obviously I can't write that, so instead I'm just writing about how Hardy uses the character of Tess to show his view that we are basically all pawns of fate. Cheery stuff.

Lawson's making us write an outline which counts for ten percent of the course grade. It sucks, because outlines totally don't work for me. Usually I don't figure out exactly what I want to say until I start writing. So I pretty much have to write at least a draft of the paper before I can write the outline. Which means I have to do the whole thing this weekend.

On the other hand, it's not like I have much else to do. At least I'm not thinking about Beth or checking her Facebook profile every hour.

After dinner, Mom drops me off at the mall. I duck inside, wait a couple of minutes and then head back out to walk the few blocks to Parker's place.

The pizza place downstairs is packed. A neon sign flashes *PIZZA PALACE* in lurid green, and the huge sign below reads *We Have 2 for 1 "slices!"* The word *slices* is in quotation marks. Like they're not really slices at all. Pseudo-slices. It reminds me of Shelley with her "start time" and "group process."

I push the door open and trek up the stairs. The voices and laughter from the pizza place fade. I knock hard on Parker's door and wait. No one answers. I'm about to knock again when the door swings open.

It is obvious from the look on Jamie's face that something is wrong. He stares at me hard, his eyes flat gray and his mouth twisted thin as barbed wire. He swears under his breath, and with a jab of one hand, gestures for me to go into the living room.

Parker is sitting on the gray carpet—they don't have much furniture—with her arms wrapped around her knees. Her face is red and blotchy and her eyes are pink-rimmed and bloodshot.

"Are you okay?" I ask.

She shakes her head and glares past me at Jamie. "No. No, I'm not fucking okay."

"Don't drag your friend into our business." Jamie walks into the kitchen, takes a beer out of the fridge and cracks it open.

I ignore him and drop to my knees beside Parker. "What's wrong?"

"Oh…Jamie quit his job at the Golden Griddle." She wipes her nose on the back of her hand like a little kid and looks up at me, wet-eyed. "So now somehow I'm supposed to pay the rent and buy food and—"

"Shut up, Parker," Jamie yells from the kitchen doorway.

"You shut up. Asshole." Parker sniffs a few times and looks like she might start crying again. She turns back to me. "I'd sell my car but I don't think I'd get fifty bucks for it. We're going to end up getting evicted. I just know it. My parents help out but not that much."

"Why did he quit?" I ask, looking from Parker to Jamie.

"He says he doesn't want to participate in that whole system. You know, money and stuff." She raises her voice. "He wants to eat though. He wants somewhere to fucking live."

"Shut up, Parker." Jamie walks over to us, his face tight and angry.

"What are you going to do, Jamie? Are you going to hit me again? In front of Dante? That'd be real nice." She spits the words out. "He's just jealous because I have a friend. You don't like me to have friends, do you, Jamie?"

My heart is pounding. I am crouching on the floor beside Parker. Jamie is towering over us. I stand up. At least I'm as tall as him. If he hits Parker, I'll kill him. I will. I imagine the feel of my fist connecting with his face, nose crunching, bone and blood. I shudder, my stomach clenching. I was a scrappy little kid, but I haven't actually hit anyone since fourth grade. "Look," I say, "maybe we should all just calm down." *We.* I sound like Shelley.

Jamie snorts. "And maybe you should get your face out of our business."

There is a knock at the door.

"Leo," Parker says. She jumps up and runs to the door.

"Hey," Leo says, stepping inside. The easy grin slips from his face and his forehead creases in concern. "What's wrong? You been crying, Parker?" He reaches a hand out as if he's about to touch her cheek but stops short and lets his hand slowly drop back down to his side. He glances from Parker, to me, to Jamie. When he speaks again, his voice is guarded. "You okay?"

She nods, not quite looking at him. "Fine. I'm fine."

There's a tense silence. Leo opens his mouth as if he's about to say something; then he closes it again. I wonder what he's thinking. After a minute, he shakes his head and turns toward Jamie. "Well, I was just over at Keenan's place. There's going to be a demo Monday morning, down in front of Central School."

"A demo? What for?" I ask.

Jamie gives me a scornful look, and I flash one back at him. *Asshole.* "What?" I say. "You don't think I should know what I'm protesting? You might be happy to jump on any excuse to get pissed off, but I actually like to have a reason."

Parker places a hand on my arm, but Leo just nods. "You know Central, right?"

I nod. It's downtown, a huge old building near the hospital, with a reputation for being a druggie school.

"Well, Keenan's friend Paul goes there, and they just kicked him out for handing out anti-war flyers."

"Seriously? They kicked him out?"

"Yeah. They called them 'unauthorized materials', like he was handing out bomb-making kits or something. Hauled him down to the office and basically interrogated him for over an hour. Then they suspended him."

"Shit." I think about Parker, handing out flyers at GRSS. "Can they do that?"

"Well, they did it, didn't they? So I guess they can."

"But what about free speech and all that? Doesn't he have a right to express his opinion?"

Jamie looks at me like he can't believe what a total idiot I am. "Duh. At school? What planet do you live on, Dante?"

He has a point. Mr. Lawson practically sends me down to the office for breathing in class. Free speech is not a big part of my life at GRSS. Still..."Can he go back? I mean, to finish his diploma?"

"Only if he signs some agreement to stop handing out flyers, and he won't do that."

"Wow. That's awful."

"So you're in? For the protest, I mean?" Leo looks at me.

"Monday morning? Um, I've got school."

Parker nudges me. "Oh, come on. You can skip one morning."

Mr. Lawson's class. On one hand, I'd like nothing better than to miss it. On the other, I obviously would not get away with it. Detentions suck. Besides, I'm supposed to hand in the outline for my paper on Monday.

"Well? We could pick you up at the corner, like last time." Her eyes are still pink-rimmed, but she's smiling at me, that crazy wide smile that's too big for her face.

I just want to see her again. Maybe I can finish the paper and the outline tomorrow and run it over to the school before classes start. "Okay," I tell her. "I'll come."

FOURTEEN

I hang out with Parker and the others until eleven;
then I sprint back to the mall to pretend that I've just
come out of the movie. Mom's car is waiting for me in the
parking lot. As soon as I get close, I can see that Dad is
with her, and I know something is wrong.

She opens the car door. "Get in."

"Thanks," I say. I slide into the backseat and buckle up,
not looking at them.

"Where were you?" Mom asks. Her voice is low and
calm. Not a good sign.

I decide to bluff. "What do you mean? I was at the
movies. You dropped me off, remember?"

Dad turns to look at me, his face creased and worried.

Mom shakes her head. "Don't *lie* to me, Emily. I had
to pick up something at the mall myself. I parked the car,
and then I saw you come out and walk down the street."

She drums her fingers on the steering wheel and waits for me to answer.

I can't think of anything to say that won't make things worse.

She raises her voice. "I tried to follow you in the car, but it was a one-way street, and by the time I got around the block, I couldn't see you anymore."

I bet she's been freaking out all night. "I'm sorry."

"I thought I could trust you." Mom's mouth tightens into a thin line. Her eyes are titanium-hard. "I can't believe you lied to me."

I bite my lip. "I really was with someone I met at the group."

"So why the charade about the mall?"

"She lives downtown," I say. "I just went to her place."

"So why not just ask me to drop you off at her house?"

I sigh. "Because she doesn't live with her parents. She lives in an apartment with her boyfriend, and I didn't think you'd let me go if I told you that."

Mom looks like she is going to explode. Her face is all red except for two tiny white lines by her nostrils. "Emily. You go on and on about how we should trust your judgment, and then you pull a stunt like this."

"See? I knew you'd have a problem with it."

"I have a problem with you lying to me and hanging out with god knows who in some dive of an apartment—"

"You're the one who wanted me to go to that stupid group. You're the one who wanted me to make friends."

"Don't try to twist this around."

I run my fingers over the back of my left hand and feel the roughness where my knuckles are still scraped up from climbing the school. "Look, Mom. I was with Parker, a girl from the social skills group. What difference does it make if we were at the mall or at her place?"

"Emily, I'm sorry but if I can't trust you to be honest about where you're going, you can't go anywhere." She lets out a long breath. "You're grounded."

Dad nods, like it's only reasonable. I'm sixteen and therefore I have to do whatever they say, whereas they can do whatever they want. And they don't *want* anything. They just go along, time ticking by, getting older, Mom agonizing about wrinkles and experimenting with new cosmetics and Dad setting up war games and cutting his food into cubes.

I can't stand it.

"Aren't you going to say anything?" Mom demands. "Well, Emily?"

"Dante," I say. "It's Dante." I stare out the window all the way home.

The next morning, I wake early but don't bother getting up. What's the point? I can't go anywhere. I finally drag myself downstairs at noon because I am starving.

I peek into the living room. Mom is scrapbooking the photographs from a vacation we took before we moved here. A lifetime ago. Glossy rectangles of beaches and Mayan

ruins litter the glass-topped coffee table, along with everything from plane tickets to menus.

She doesn't look up, and I have no desire for a heart-
to-heart chat about last night, so I make myself some toast
and grab an apple from the fruit bowl on the counter. I'm
about to go back upstairs with my food when the phone
rings.

I look at it, hesitating. Mom gets up and comes into the
kitchen to answer it.

"Hello?" Her eyebrows shoot up. "Yes. Just a minute."
She passes it to me and taps her watch. "Two minutes."

This is part of my parents' version of grounding—
time limits on calls, no phone in my room, no TV and no
Internet.

I take the phone from her. "Hello?"

"Dante? It's Leo."

Mom is standing about six inches from me, and I bet she
can hear every word. I step away and turn my back. "Hi."

"Hey. I was just wondering what you were up to
tonight. Paul and Keenan are having a party, nothing huge,
just a few friends. Want to come?"

"I don't think I can."

"Really? That's too bad." He sounds disappointed.
"Can't you come for a bit, even? I could pick you up. We're
going early, to make some signs and stuff for Monday's
demo."

I'm pretty sure he likes me. It would be so easy if I
could like him back. I glance at Mom. She's standing by
the island, carefully rearranging the fruit in the bowl,

which apparently I disturbed by removing an apple. "I'm grounded," I tell him.

"Shit. How come?"

"Long story." I don't want to explain in front of Mom, which is kind of stupid since obviously she already knows why.

"Ah. Can't talk?"

"Right." I wonder what Leo's thinking. None of his friends have to deal with parents. Keenan and Paul obviously have their own place, like Jamie and Parker. I wonder if Leo lives alone or if he has roommates or anything. Maybe he has a girlfriend, although you'd think I'd know that by now. I want to ask him if we're still on for Monday but I can't. "So...," I say, wanting him to keep talking.

"Man. Your folks keep you on a pretty short leash, huh?"

"Yeah, I guess." I glance across at Mom and she taps her watch. I lower my voice. "Um, is Parker okay? She seemed kind of upset last night."

Leo pauses, like he's considering his answer. "It's not the first time. She's...well, she's a complicated girl, Dante."

"Yeah, but..."

"She'll be fine," he says. "They fight sometimes but they always seem to work it out, you know?"

I don't know. Personally, I think Jamie's a jerk, and from what Parker said, it sounded like he'd hit her. I think she should dump his sorry ass. I think Leo and I should be helping her pack her stuff. But I don't say any of that.

Mom clears her throat and taps her watch again.

"I better go," I say reluctantly.

"Well, I'll see you Monday then. You're still up for that, right?"

"Absolutely." I put the phone down with a click.

"Who was that?" Mom asks.

"A friend." I reach deep into the carefully rearranged fruit bowl and pull out a pear. "Changed my mind," I say, putting the apple back on top of the now crooked pile. Then I smile brightly at Mom and head upstairs.

Monday morning, I tell Mom I'm going in early. I run all the way to school and I'm at Mrs. Greenway's office at eight o'clock. I hand the secretary my outline and ask her to please give it to Mr. Lawson first thing. I figure he'd love to fail me. No way am I going to give him an excuse to do it.

I walk down the empty hallway. It's clean and silent and smells like bleach. I step into the washroom for a pee; then I wash my hands and face and look at my reflection in the mirror. The front of my T-shirt is a V of sweat. I wish I'd brought a clean one to change into.

I hate it here. I hate everything about this school: the shiny green and blue lockers, the kitschy artwork on the walls, the never-quite-erased chalkboards, the green metal garbage cans, the locker room smell that the bleach can't completely hide.

I walk down the empty hallway and wish I was leaving forever instead of just skipping one morning. My heart is racing and I keep half expecting Mrs. G. or some teacher to pounce on me and ask me where I'm going. I make it outside and take one last look back at the building. *GRSS: The tenth circle of hell.* Dante Alighieri's demons had nothing on Mr. Lawson and his ilk. I'd take heat, high winds and hornet stings over the petty rules and excruciating boredom of this place. I blow out a long breath, trying to steady myself. Then I jog slowly all the way back to the corner and wait for Parker and Leo and Jamie to pick me up.

They arrive about two minutes after I get there, Leo's car rattling down the wide lawn-edged road.

"You know what I hate about school?" I say, getting in the car. "I hate the color of the washrooms. Who would choose that color, unless they actually wanted to be unkind to the inmates? Seriously."

Jamie rolls his eyes, like he can't believe I am so petty and small-minded.

Parker giggles. "What color is it?"

I picture it. It's a revolting shade that hovers some-where between pink, orange and beige. "Hard to describe," I say. "Okay, you know what it is? Imagine if you ate a can of ravioli, followed it with a glass of milk, and then threw up. That's the color."

Leo gives an appreciative chuckle. "Puke Pink. Nice."

"They were pale green at my school," Parker says in a low voice. "Institutional, you know? Hospital green."

Her jaw tightens and she ducks her head, fumbling for her smokes. "I hate that color."

There's something about her voice that makes me shiver, and I wonder if she's been in a hospital or something. I don't feel like I can ask though, not in front of the guys. "You ever heard of Dante Alighieri?" I say instead.

She shakes her head.

"He was an Italian guy, like seven hundred years ago. He wrote this long poem called the *Divine Comedy*. You've heard of Dante's *Inferno*, right?"

She nods.

"Well, that's part of it. It's pretty cool. It's about this guy—well, Dante himself—who travels through hell and purgatory and heaven, and describes it all. Hell is divided into these circles, nine circles, with different kinds of sinners ending up in different places."

"Are you named after him?" Parker asks.

"Yeah. Well, I chose the name, but that's why."

Jamie cuts me off. "Don't tell me you're a Bible-thumper."

"No, no." I shake my head quickly. "It's not like that. I mean, I don't believe in this. I don't take it literally, you know? I just like it."

He looks at me like I'm nuts. "If you don't believe in it, what's the point?"

"I don't know." I shouldn't have brought it up with Jamie here. I bet Parker would have liked it, if I'd waited, but anything I say now will sound stupid.

Leo turns down the music. "It's a metaphor, right?"

Inferno

I look at him gratefully. "Yeah, that's right. Or, um, what's the word? An allegory."

"Listen to you two," Parker says. "I feel like I'm back in school."

She looks interested though, so I keep talking. "I love the idea that hell is almost this orderly place, with these circles and rules and gateways and guards. Monster guards, granted, but still."

"Yeah, that's cool. Hey, I made it out without getting lost this time." Leo turns onto the highway and speeds up. It sounds like the car needs a new muffler. "I don't think I could read all that heaven and hell stuff though. My parents are into all that. They're the insurance policy type of Christians, you know? Like, we better say we believe it and show up at church once a week in case it's really true. I don't suppose they ever think about God or what any of it means, but they don't want to risk burning in hell." He shrugs. "It's hypocritical, but at least they're not crazy religious like Parker's folks."

A clue about Parker's family. I file it away to ask her about later.

"People are scared shitless of chaos," Leo says. "That's why everyone thinks anarchists are bad or messed up. Like if there was no government telling us what to do, we'd all run around killing each other or something." He laughs. "It'd be funny if my parents got to hell and it turned out it wasn't chaotic at all, but more like some kind of crazy bureaucracy."

"Yeah." I nod. "With Satan in charge of the whole hierarchy."

"Satan as the CEO."

"Or the principal," Parker says.

I laugh. "Handing out detentions. Yo, sinner—I hear you ate a whole pizza. Go spend a week in the third circle with the gluttons."

"What happens to the gluttons?" Parker asks.

I frown, trying to remember. "I think they had to wade through stinky frozen slush or something. Or lie in it, maybe. Cerberus guards them anyway. He's a three-headed dog and he snaps at them if they try to get away."

"Nice." Leo slows down as he exits the highway and turns onto King Street. "Almost there."

Jamie hasn't said a word. He's in the passenger seat, facing forward, but I don't have to see his face to know he's pissed off. I look over at Parker and she grins at me. Under her left eye, a dark purple streak fades into light blue-gray. A bruise.

She sees me looking and her grin slips from her face. She shakes her head ever so slightly, warning me not to say anything. As if I would. I turn away from her and stare at the back of Jamie's head. I wouldn't mind siccing Cerberus on him.

FIFTEEN

There are a ton of people milling around in front of Central when we arrive, and for a moment I think this protest is going to be huge. Then I realize that most of them are just Central students heading to class like they do every day.

Jamie lifts some cardboard signs out of the back of the station wagon and drops them on the ground. *NO FREE SPEECH AT CENTRAL*, the top one reads. "Here, guys," he says. "Stick these up anywhere you can. And if anyone asks you what you're doing, see if you can get them to join the protest. We want the classrooms to be empty. That should get their attention."

He flags down a passing student, a serious-looking girl carrying a stack of books. "Hey, you know your school doesn't recognize your right to free speech?"

She looks at him like he's crazy and keeps on walking. Jamie strides off into the crowd, handing out flyers and talking to anyone who will listen. Leo grabs a stack of signs and follows him, heading toward the front doors of the school.

I look at Parker, feeling oddly disengaged from what is going on.

She tucks her thumbs through her belt loops. "So."

"So." I reach out and almost touch her cheek, the bruise there, but pull my hand back at the last minute. "What happened?"

"Nothing. It was just stupid."

"He hit you, didn't he?"

Parker doesn't deny it. She just watches me with those pale eyes and says nothing.

"I knew it. That asshole." I clench my fists, feeling the nails dig into my palms.

She's quiet for a moment. "When all this stuff was going on with my family last year and I was such a mess...I don't know. He was the only one who even tried to understand what I was going through."

I try not to roll my eyes. "Okay. Fine. Points for Jamie. But that doesn't mean he gets to treat you like dirt now."

"No. He doesn't though. Not all the time. You see his worst side." She looks at me thoughtfully. "He doesn't like you very much."

"It's mutual. Sorry."

"Whatever." She picks up some signs. "We're supposed to hang around by the doors and talk to students. Try and talk them out of going to class."

"We're supposed to?"

"Well, Leo says." She looks at me, considering. "What's up with you and him anyway?"

"Me and *Leo*? Nothing's up."

Parker watches my face for a long moment, and I can feel my cheeks getting hot. She shrugs. "Well, whatever you say." She starts walking toward the school.

"Um, why did you ask?" I grab a sign and follow her, glancing down at it as I walk. *How Many Lives per Gallon?* it reads in blocky black letters. "Did Leo say something?"

"Aha." She stops and turns to face me. "I knew it."

I don't want to lie to her, and besides, maybe she already knows. "Okay. So when we hung the sign from the roof last week, it was kind of intense. And Leo kissed me. Once, for about three seconds. But that is absolutely it. End of story. Nothing is going on with us."

"I'm pretty sure he likes you."

"You think?"

"Mm-hmm. Are you interested? He's a good guy, Dante. A real sweetheart." She winks. "If I was single, I'd be all over him."

I stop walking because we're getting close to the school and I can see Jamie standing twenty feet away talking to a group of girls. "No," I say. "Not really." I can hardly say what I'm thinking, which is that I'm more interested in Parker. Not much point having a crush on a straight girl.

"Are you sure? I know he's a bit intense but he's cute, don't you think? And he's the kind of guy who wouldn't let you down, you know? He's the kind of guy who'd always be there for you."

I wonder why she isn't with him instead of Jamie.

"Come on," she coaxes. "Tell me what you think."

I force myself to think about Leo. He's intelligent and interesting, and I like talking to him. And it sure would be easier to go out with a guy. Mom would be happy. Well, sort of happy anyway. Except for the fact that he doesn't go to school or have a job. "I don't know," I say. "I don't think so, Parker. Who does he live with anyway? Does he have his own place?"

She looks surprised. "I figured you knew. He lives with his parents. Helps take care of his mom."

"What's wrong with her?"

"Some kind of disability. Can't remember what it's called. Not MS but it's something that is only going to get worse."

It doesn't fit with the mental image I had of his parents heading off to church every week in their Sunday clothes. A picture drifts into my mind of Leo helping a frail but attractive woman out of a wheelchair, sitting beside her while she knits in the evenings. It's an image right out of some tearjerker made-for-TV movie. Probably the reality is nothing like that. For all I know, his mom is morbidly obese and spends her evenings smoking cigars and playing video games. I don't really know Leo at all.

"What about your parents, Parker?" I ask. "What are they like?"

"Assholes," she says succinctly. "Come on. We better get to work."

We walk around, sticking up posters on the school wall and on parking-lot signs, and trying to persuade Central students to stay out of class in protest. Jamie keeps yelling, "No Free Speech at Central!" People stare at him, curious, but mostly they just go inside anyway. A couple of girls tell me that Paul is a weirdo and they don't care if he gets kicked out. A guy demands to know where he is, and I have to admit Paul hasn't actually shown up yet, which he thinks is pretty hilarious.

The thing is, even though I think it's terrible to kick a student out for protesting the war, I'm having a hard time getting into this. I'm not scared of getting in trouble— I mean, I don't go to this school, so what can they do to me?—but I'm finding it a bit embarrassing. Maybe if there were more of us, it'd be okay. It'd help if Jamie would stop yelling. As it is though, I'm squirming with self-conscious-ness. The stealthy, middle-of-the-night adrenaline rush of hanging the sign at GRSS was more my style.

Finally the bell rings. It's ten to nine. We've managed to stick up a fair number of posters and, amazingly, to avoid the attention of teachers. On the other hand, we haven't convinced any Central students to join us. Parker, Leo and I stand around for a few minutes, holding up our signs, even though no one is looking, and waiting to see if anything is going to happen. I think Jamie is hoping a teacher will come out—he's pacing back and forth and looks ready for a fight.

A car pulls in to the parking lot and veers to a crooked stop in front of the doors.

"Bit late now," Jamie says. "Typical."

A red-haired guy gets out of the driver seat, and seven others somehow emerge from the small car.

"Sorry we're late," the red-haired guy says. He has reddish skin, lots of piercings and very bright blue eyes. He rubs his forehead and looks embarrassed. "We overslept."

Jamie doesn't say anything. His face is expressionless, but I can tell he's angry. I can feel it radiating from him, like heat or light, and I find myself stepping away slightly.

Parker fills the silence. "Keenan, this is our friend, Dante. I told you about her."

He nods to me. "Hey. Yeah, I heard about your stunt at GRSS. Climbing the school. Pretty impressive."

The sign he's holding says *War Is Failure*. I'm a bit confused about whether this is an anti-war demonstration or a protest against the school's decision to suspend a student for protesting war. I think we might have had more success getting Central students to walk out if we'd been a little clearer and stayed focused on what their own school had done, but I bite my tongue. It's not like I was there to help plan it anyway.

"This is pointless," Jamie says. "Classes have started. They're just ignoring us."

"Everyone going in read the signs," I point out. "That's got to have made them more aware of what happened. And we talked to lots of people."

"Didn't manage to convince any to walk out though," Jamie says.

I wonder if he really imagined that we'd get a whole school to walk out. I could've told him it wasn't likely. "Most people aren't going to do that." I turn and look at Leo. "No matter what we do. They're too much, you know...in their own worlds."

"Half awake," Leo agrees. He keeps his eyes on my face in that way he has, as if there isn't a bunch of other people standing right here with us, as if it's just me and him alone somewhere. I can feel my cheeks getting hot. I wish Parker hadn't said anything about him liking me. I want to be friends with him and now I feel all...uncomfortable. If he starts getting some stupid crush on me, it'll mess everything up. Granted, I have an equally stupid crush on Parker, but at least I have the sense to keep it to myself.

Jamie's words break into my thoughts. "We need to do something to wake them up," he says, his voice hard-edged. "Something big. Something that'll get everyone's attention."

A flicker of uneasiness prickles at the back of my neck. "Maybe we could do the sign thing again," I say quickly. "I mean, hanging a sign from the roof. Do one here at Central, saying *No Free Speech in School*. Or, you know, something better but along those lines."

Keenan looks at the school doubtfully, and I follow his gaze. Three stories high, a sheer red-brick wall with a definite shortage of ledges and windowsills. I imagine being up there, clinging to the bricks, body pressed against the wall. My hands are instantly wet and I wipe them on my jeans as I turn back to face the others.

They're all staring at the wall and Leo is nodding slowly. "Maybe," he says. "That's not a bad idea."

Parker touches my arm. "Dante...are you sure you want to do that? It looks, well, it's really high." She bites her lower lip. "I don't want you to get hurt."

"Don't be such a wuss," Jamie says.

I scowl at him. It's not like he's the one taking the risks.

"She can do it," Leo says confidently. "I'm telling you guys, she can climb. Spider Girl. Right, Dante?"

"Right," I say. There is an awful sick feeling in my stomach, but I ignore it. I know this is crazy but I'm remembering the feeling I had after I climbed GRSS. I felt like I could do anything—like nothing mattered, not school, not Mr. Lawson, not Beth. I want that feeling back again. I look at the others and nod. "Right."

SIXTEEN

Leo drives me back to GRSS. It's the last place I want to be right now, but I don't know what else to do. Parker keeps looking across the backseat at me, all worried, the bruise on her cheek vivid against her pale skin. My mind feels oddly blank, and my stomach is in knots.

"I'll call you," she says as I get out of the car.

I nod vaguely and walk into the school.

Mrs. G. waves me over as I walk past the office. I sigh and walk in. "Hi, Mrs. G."

"Have a seat," she says.

I flop into the chair, feeling suddenly exhausted. "I guess I need a late pass."

She glances at her watch. "It's almost ten. What's up?"

Nothing I can tell her about, that's for sure. "I don't want to be here," I hear myself say. "I'm thinking about quitting."

"You are too smart, way too smart, to mess up your education," she says. "What do you want to do, Dante?

I mean, you want to get into university, right?"

"I guess I do." It all seems such a long way off.

She swivels her chair around and rummages in a filing cabinet. She pulls out a cream-colored file folder and flips through its contents. "You were a straight-A student when you came here. Last year, mostly *As* except for English and socials. Despite a fair number of detentions. And this year...well, it's only been a couple of weeks, but you've been in my office several times, Mr. Lawson says you're disruptive in class..."

I sit forward, stung. "Disruptive? That's so not fair. He just doesn't like me."

She sighs. "You skipped class last week and again today, and now you're talking about dropping out."

I stare at the file folder. I thought she was on my side, but it sounds like she's just taking Mr. Lawson's word for everything.

"I'd like you to talk to the school counselor, Dante. Would you do that?"

I imagine someone like Shelley asking me how I *really* feel about school. "Do I have to? I mean, I don't have anything to talk about."

She purses her lips and plays with the long beaded chain that her reading glasses hang from. "Is everything okay at home?"

"Fine." Teachers always do this. Trying to shift responsibility somewhere else. They can't grasp that maybe it isn't home that's the problem. It's school. It's them.

"Then..."

"I told you. I hate it here. It's like a prison. And Mr. Lawson acts like a prison guard, always throwing his power around." I know it's a mistake as soon as I say it, but the words just slip out.

Mrs. G. watches me closely for a long minute. Neither of us speak. Finally, she closes my file folder, turns and puts it away. When she swivels back to face me again, her face is unreadable. "Dante, I'm not going to ask if you had anything to do with the sign that appeared on the roof earlier this week. But if you did, I'd suggest you think carefully about what you are doing. Very carefully."

I guess the prison guard comment wasn't too smart. "Mrs. G…" I don't know what I want to say.

She shakes her head and points to the clock. "You'd better get to your next class."

All day I sit in classroom after classroom and feel like I'm in a fog. Every single teacher gives us pointless, repetitive, busy work, none of which interests me in the least. It's like they see our minds as empty space for them to cram full of so-called knowledge. No one seems to entertain the possibility that we might actually be capable of thinking for ourselves.

I draw Dante Alighieri's monsters on the cover of my binder—three-headed Cerberus; snaky Geryon; Charon, ancient and flaming-eyed, ferrying Dante across the river and into hell. I don't know what to do. I'm just going through the motions here. This place is a factory, and all graduation means is that you drop off the end of the conveyor belt. I don't want to spend the rest of my life flipping burgers—or pancakes, for that matter—but I can't imagine getting through another two years of this bullshit.

Of course, if I fall from halfway up the wall of Central, it won't matter what I decide. Splat. Game over.

At afternoon break, Linnea grabs me. "Come for a smoke?"

"I don't smoke," I remind her, but I follow her outside anyway.

Linnea walks across the field and sits down on the grass beside one of the new spindly trees. I sit down too, wondering what she wants. We've always been friendly but in a slightly distant way.

She lights a joint and offers it to me. I shake my head but smile so she doesn't think I'm being snotty about it.

"So...," she says. She inhales and holds the smoke in for a few seconds before blowing it out slowly in a thin gray cloud.

"So," I say, "what's up?"

"Um, look. If I've got this wrong, don't freak on me, okay?"

"Okay." *It's about Beth*, I think, remembering the comment she made last week: *I heard you guys were real close.*

She lifts her chin and brushes her hair off her face, so for once I can see both her eyes. "I heard that you and Beth were, you know, together."

"Beth has a boyfriend," I say quickly. I don't know why—she's hundreds of miles away—but I feel protective of her. She'd hate for anyone to know.

Linnea doesn't say anything for a moment. She takes another drag, watching me through the smoke. Then she shrugs. "Well, whatever. I guess maybe this wouldn't interest you then."

"What wouldn't?"

"I'm trying to start some kind of group, you know, for queer students."

"Here? I mean, at GRSS?" It's hard to imagine.

"Mrs. Greenway agreed to it and all. For support, right? And to try to make some changes in attitudes." She grimaces. "People here are pretty homophobic, you know? I guess you've probably noticed. This school is stuck in the nineties."

"Yeah, it is. At my old school, lots of students were totally out. Well, not lots, but a few. These two guys used to walk around practically holding hands. They did a freaking duet together at a school talent show. Can you imagine that happening here?"

"They'd be killed," she says flatly. "Seriously."

I think about Beth and how scared she was, how she couldn't even admit to herself that we were more than just friends. Even if there had been a support group, she wouldn't have gone anywhere near it.

"Anyway, I just thought I'd tell you, you know, in case…" Linnea's voice trails off.

"I'm not really the support-group type," I say, avoiding the question she hasn't quite asked. "It sounds like a cool idea though. I mean, good luck with it, okay?"

"Oh. Okay." She chews on her bottom lip and looks like she wishes she'd never brought it up.

Up until today, I'd always assumed Linnea was straight. She still hasn't actually come right out and said she's not, but presumably that's what all this is about. I sort of wish I could talk to her, but I can't say anything, not without talking about Beth. I feel kind of bad because she took a risk to tell me about the group, and I haven't given her anything back. I cross my legs and lean toward her. "Actually," I tell her, "I'm thinking about dropping out anyway."

"Ahh, don't do that." She puts out the joint by pinching it between her finger and thumb, and sticks it in her pocket. "You gotta finish grade twelve. Two more years, you can do that. You know, I read that studies show high school graduates earn forty-eight percent more than non-graduates."

I raise my eyebrows. Who'd have thought Linnea, who drifts through every day in a THC-induced daze, would be trying to persuade me to stay in school? I grin at her. "Yeah, but studies show that people who leave high school early are fifty-two percent happier than those who stick around."

Her hair has fallen back over half her face, a shiny dark shield. "You're shitting me. Really? Did they really show that?"

I sigh. "No," I admit. "I just made that up."

We sit there in silence for a moment. I stare down the row of trees and wonder, if I stay for two more years, how much they'll have grown. I really do want my grade-twelve diploma. I'm pretty sure I even want to go to university. To do English, go figure. Mr. Lawson wouldn't believe it, but it's true.

I just don't know if I can stick it out for long enough to get there.

"Hey, Linnea?"

"Mm?"

"You've gone to GRSS since grade nine, right?"

She nods. "Sad but true."

"So…you never knew a guy called Leo, did you? He would've been in grade eleven when you were in grade nine, but he quit halfway through the year."

"Doesn't sound familiar. But grade nine…I was still sort of doing my best to blend in with the walls, you know? I didn't notice anyone outside of myself." Linnea shakes her head. "I could ask my brother though. If Leo went here, they'd probably have been in some of the same classes." She looks at me curiously. "So who is he?"

"Just a guy," I tell her.

"Boyfriend?"

"No." I take a deep breath. "Um, so about your group? I'll think about it."

After school I go for a long, long run. Mom approves of exercise, so it's one of the few things I'm allowed to do when I'm grounded. I run down Willow Terrace to Oak Place, turn onto Maple and then run all the way along Lilac Avenue. I run past the driveways with their suvs, past the double and triple garages, past the kids playing street hockey and riding their bikes in aimless circles, past the emptied and neatly inverted recycling boxes waiting to be taken inside when everyone comes home from work. I run my usual six-mile route, but I don't want to stop. I run right past my house, run until my chest is bursting and my legs are screaming to stop.

I finally stagger to a halt at a small playground over-looking the highway. A couple of kids eye me curiously, their half-melted Popsicles dripping orange and purple ooze onto the grass. I'm breathing hard and I bet my face is bright red. I ignore the kids and climb to the top of an empty aluminum climbing frame, where I sit at the top of the red plastic slide with my legs hanging down. I should stretch, but I don't. I just sit and concentrate on the feel of my heart beating.

Slowly, the kids trickle away, called back to their houses by the smells of dinner. The sun slips from the sky and disappears behind the rows of houses, and the sky turns from blue to dark gray. Down on the highway, cars turn on their headlights, and all around me, suvs pull into drive-ways and lights go on in living rooms. Even here, with the lawns mowed within an inch of their lives and the swimming pool filters buzzing like a chorus of crickets, the world has its own weird beauty.

I should go home, but I sit for a few minutes longer, drumming my heels against the plastic slide and listening to the hollow thudding noise they make. *Thumpety-thump.* Like my heart beating.

I sit for a moment, poised on the top of the slide; then I push off, flying down to land on my feet in the sand below.

Climbing the wall at Central would border on suicidal.

When I get home, Mom's waiting in the kitchen, looking pissed off.

"I went for a run," I say quickly.

"For two hours?"

"Yeah, actually."

She just looks at me.

"I did. I swear."

She keeps staring at me, all suspicious. I grab a glass from the cupboard and notice that my hand is trembling. I pour a glass of water from the tap, drink it fast and refill it.

"There's filtered water in the fridge, you know." She sounds annoyed.

"Whatever." I drink a second glass; then I turn to go up to my room. "I have to make a call."

"No phone calls from your room," she says automatically. "In case you've forgotten, you're grounded."

I groan. "Mom…It's important."

"Then call from the kitchen. Two minutes." She points to the phone.

Like I can have this conversation in front of her. But maybe I can figure out a way to tell Parker and the others that I need to talk to them. I pick up the phone and dial Leo's cell number.

The voice mail picks up. Leo's voice. "Leave a message if you want to and I'll call you back if I want to."

"Hi," I say, thinking fast. "It's Dante. I guess you're not there, so I'll see you tomorrow at school. If I don't see you before homeroom, I'll meet you at lunchtime by the main doors." I hang up and look at my mother. "There. Satisfied?"

"Who was that?"

"No one. A machine."

"I gathered that. Whose machine?"

"Jeez, Mom. Can't I have any privacy?"

She purses her mouth tightly, the skin wrinkling in tiny vertical creases. "Not if I can't trust you to tell me the truth."

"Fine," I say. "It was Linnea. A girl from school."

"Oh. Well. Good." She tilts her head to one side. "A new friend?"

"Sort of. Not really. I've known her for a while." I have a fleeting urge to tell Mom that Linnea's a total stoner who wants me to get involved with this queer group she's starting, but for once I manage to hold my tongue. Mrs. G. would be proud.

SEVENTEEN

I don't see Leo or the others before school. Mr. Lawson tries to bait me into an argument during homeroom by making snarky comments about my hair and by calling me Emily, but I refuse to be drawn in. I absolutely can't get a lunch-hour detention today.

When the bell rings at ten to twelve, I'm out the door in a flash.

Parker is standing right where she was the first time I met her, wearing the same faded skinny jeans and multicolored sweater. I grin, and then I notice that she's not alone. Leo and Jamie are there too.

"Hey. Sorry about the cryptic message," I tell Leo. "Mom was standing about two feet from the phone."

He nods. "Yeah, I figured."

"I'm not going to do that climb," I say, speaking fast so I can't change my mind. "At Central, you know? It's too hard. Too dangerous."

"Good," Parker says quickly. "Good. It's so not worth risking your life over, you know?"

"Really? You're not going to?" Jamie's eyes shift from me to Parker, to Leo and back to me. Then he smiles ever so slightly. "Well, don't worry about it. I've got another plan anyway."

"You do?" Parker looks surprised. "With Paul and Keenan and those guys?"

"No. Forget those guys. They couldn't even show up on time at Central. This is just us. No one else."

"What is? What are you talking about?" She shifts her weight from one foot to the other, agitated. Anxious.

Jamie steps away from the doors and gestures for us to follow. When we get to the edge of the grassy field, he stops and turns to face us. "We need to decide when and where to do it."

"Do what?" I ask. "What's the plan?"

There is a long silence.

"I want to know if you're in first," he says. "We don't want anyone wussing out."

"What about me? You haven't told me either." Parker wraps her arms around herself as if she's cold.

Leo looks at me. "You're in, aren't you, Dante? You're with us?"

"Sure," I say. "Why not? As long as I don't have to climb any three-story buildings."

He looks at Jamie. "Good enough?"

Jamie shrugs. "Whatever."

"What about me?" Parker says again. "Don't you want to make sure I'm in too?"

"You're in," Jamie says flatly.

I look at Parker. She drops her eyes and doesn't say anything.

"So what's the plan?" I ask, trying to keep my voice light.

"This is something I've been thinking about for a while," Jamie says. He turns and looks at Leo.

Leo clears his throat. For once, he isn't meeting my eyes. "The thing is, a lot of our actions—handing out flyers at the schools or the protest yesterday, for example—haven't accomplished much."

"I don't know about that. It made me think. I mean, if it wasn't for Parker's flyers, I wouldn't be here."

Jamie snorts. "Yeah. One person out of a whole school."

"Still, that's a start," I say, remembering what Parker had said about change happening one person at a time.

Jamie ignores me. "The sign you and Leo hung up at GRSS—Parker said you told her no one even talked about it."

"Yeah." I nod. "But if we did something like that again...or maybe handed out those flyers about schools and prisons..."

He shakes his head and smiles. "Nah. We need to do something that'll get their attention."

He and Leo look at each other, and for a moment no one says anything. Parker's eyes meet mine. She looks scared, and I feel a sudden chill, a prickling at the back of my neck and a gripping tightness in my belly. Whatever is going to be said next, I'm not sure I want to hear it.

Jamie drops his cigarette and grinds it under his heel. "Leo didn't have a good time here, did you, Leo?"

There's something in his voice—something hard and taunting—that makes me shiver.

Leo shakes his head. "Don't go there, Jamie."

"Aww...bad memories?"

"Stop it." Parker's voice is sharp.

There is a tense silence. A standoff of some kind. I look from Jamie to Leo, to Parker, and wonder what is going on. Finally Leo sighs, giving in. "Okay. No. I didn't have a good time here."

Jamie grins; then he lets him off the hook and turns to me. "And you don't much like it, do you, Dante?"

He's leading me somewhere, leading all of us, and I'm not sure I want to follow. I just shake my head slowly. "Not much."

"So GRSS is our target then."

I roll my eyes. "Enough with the mystery, Jamie. What are you talking about?"

He grins. "We're going to burn your school down, Dante. That should get their fucking attention."

"You're not serious," I say. I should be shocked but mostly what I feel is disappointment. I've been so caught up in the excitement of trying to make change, so inspired by Parker and the others, and now this. It's not what I thought we were all about.

"I'm dead serious."

"It's a stupid idea," I say. "No way am I doing that."

Jamie gives a snort of disgust. "I fucking knew you'd wuss out."

I ignore him and look at Leo. "Come on, Leo. You can't honestly think this is a good idea."

He meets my eyes and his voice is low and intense. "I wasn't sure at first either, but you know, it's like Jamie says. We can't let fear stop us. If we want to make change, we have to take action."

"How the hell is burning down the school going to change anything?" I shake my head. "It'll make us look crazy. No one will take anything we say seriously."

Parker nods. "She's right. We'd be better to keep doing the stuff we were doing. Asking questions, trying to make people think."

"You're just scared," Jamie says, his voice cutting. "And so is Dante."

"We're not in grade two, Jamie," I tell him, scowling. "I'm not going to do something stupid just to prove I'm not scared."

Parker doesn't say anything.

"You're scared," Jamie says, taunting.

I stand up. "Look, I'm not scared, because I'm not doing it. It's messed up. There's no point."

His eyes are hard. "You said you were in."

"Yeah, well, I assumed you were planning something that made sense."

"You better go then," he says. "And once you're out, you're out."

Leo is watching me. His dark eyes are hard to read, and he doesn't say anything. I feel sad, like something important is ending. We'd had a connection of some sort. I'd liked being part of a group, this group. And now it's all over.

"Dante," Parker says suddenly.

I turn toward her and something catches inside me. If I'm out of the group, what does that mean for me and Parker? I don't want to lose her. "What?" I say.

She stares at me mutely.

"Parker? What is it?"

She stands there, all huddled up and swollen-eyed and miserable in her too-big sweater. The bruise on her cheek is fading and turning green. "Nothing," she says at last.

Jamie puts his arm around her protectively. Possessively. I look at her for a few seconds longer, wishing that I knew the right words to reach her. *Dump him, Parker. Walk away. Get your own life.* I swallow and say nothing. Then Parker drops her eyes, and I turn and walk away.

After school, I go down to the basement. Dad's little guys are all set up down there, rows of tiny plastic soldiers ready to fight, displays of perfect order amidst the chaos of the basement: boxes piled against the walls, stacks of furniture that Dad won't get rid of but Mom won't allow upstairs, overflowing shelves of books that I think I might re-read someday. I sit on an old wooden stool and think about my life, and about my school, and about Parker. Most of all, about Parker.

I don't know what to do.

Eventually, I hear Mom come in the front door. "Dante?"

"Down here," I yell, and then I hear her feet on the stairs.

She looks around, her nose wrinkled with displeasure. She hardly ever comes down to the basement. "What are you up to tonight?" she asks. "Homework?"

"I guess."

"Anything due tomorrow?"

I shake my head. "Nothing major." Just an English paper for Lawson, and a ton of math I've been ignoring and getting further and further behind on.

The phone rings and Mom sprints back up the stairs to answer it. "Dante," she calls. "It's for you."

I follow her up to the kitchen, wondering if it's Parker. Hoping it's Parker. Mom hands me the phone and taps her watch. "Two minutes."

"Hello," I say, ignoring her.

"It's me. Parker."

I look at my mother, willing her to leave the room. Nope.

"Hi," I say, lowering my voice. "How are you doing?"

"Dante...Look, I wanted to tell you." Her breath catches. "That thing about burning the school down? They're going to do it tonight."

I feel like she's just kicked me in the chest. My heart

is racing and my hands are sweaty, but Mom's eyes are on me, so I try to sound calm. "Really?"

"Yeah. Really. I'm outside at a pay phone. Jamie doesn't know I'm calling you."

"What about you?" I ask.

There is a pause. I picture Parker standing in the glass phone booth, twiddling the phone cord between her fingers or smoking a cigarette.

"I don't want to do it," she says at last.

"So don't."

I can hear her breathing.

"Parker? If you don't want to, then don't."

"I have to," she says. Her voice breaks. "Jamie and Leo…well, they're kind of like my family."

Mom looks at me and taps her watch again.

"Parker?" I say quickly.

"What?"

"What time? Tell me what time."

"Leo's picking us up at midnight. Dante…I'm glad you're not coming, you know? I mean, you're right, it's stupid. Worse than stupid. It's an awful thing to do." She is crying now. "But I kind of wish you were coming too."

Mom reaches for the phone, and I turn away from her, holding on tightly.

"Parker. Don't go with them," I say. "Don't." I can hear her starting to cry harder on the other end of the line.

"Dante." Mom's voice is firm and self-righteous. "That's your two minutes. Hang it up or I'll do it for you."

"Mom, this is important."

Her hand closes over mine.

"Parker, I have to go." I press End and practically throw the phone at my mother. I don't think I've ever been so angry. Right now, I almost hate her.

She looks a bit stunned. "You know the rules."

"Yeah. And she was crying and needed to talk to someone," I say. "And I just hung up on her. Thanks a lot, Mom. Real nice."

"Well, I didn't know." She hesitates. "It wasn't anything serious though, right?"

"Of course not, Mom. We're teenagers." My voice comes out really loud, but I can't seem to help it. "We don't have serious problems. Not like adults. Our problems don't matter at all."

"Calm down," she says. "Tell me what's going on. If it is really something serious, you could always call her back."

"No, I couldn't," I spit. "She doesn't have a phone."

"What was she upset about?"

For about half a second, I let myself imagine telling her. *Well, her abusive boyfriend and his pal are going to burn down my school tonight.*

"It's none of your business," I tell her.

She sighs. "Well, if it's really that important I'm sure she'll call back."

I go up to my room and try to convince myself that Leo and Jamie won't really do it. That Leo, at least, has more sense.

Call back, Parker. Call back. A second later, the phone rings, and I leap off my bed, race downstairs and meet Mom at the kitchen door. She looks at me, eyebrows raised, and I jump on the phone.

"Parker?"

"Um. No, it's Linnea."

"Oh." I'm disappointed, then surprised, and then curious. We talk at school, but she's never called me before. "What's up?"

"Look…this is none of my business, but I just thought I should call."

I watch Mom watching me from across the kitchen. "Um, is this about that group? Because I haven't really had a chance to think about that."

"No." She hesitates. "It's just, I asked my brother about that guy. Leo?"

I glance at the clock. Two minutes. "And? Did he know him?"

"Yeah. Well, he knew of him." She lowers her voice. "It sounds like Leo was bullied in grade nine. Like, really bad. Eric—that's my brother—says a group of guys kicked the shit out of him pretty regularly. Used to do stuff to humiliate him, you know? He says it was pretty sick."

"Seriously? You sure it's the same guy?"

"Yeah. Well, I guess there could be two Leos who both left at the same time." She sounds skeptical, and I have to admit it isn't likely. But neither is the image of Leo getting beat up. I can't imagine him being that vulnerable, somehow. But this would have been almost four years ago.

I guess everyone's pretty vulnerable at fourteen.

No wonder he dropped out.

"Eric says when Leo came back in grade ten, he was totally different. Like he grew a lot over the summer, and he beat the shit out of one of the guys who used to bully him. Broke his jawbone so the guy had to have it wired shut for, like, half the term."

"Jeez."

"Yeah. Eric says the other kids left Leo alone after that. Plus he'd started dealing drugs and stuff, and so he was at all the parties."

"Huh." I look at the clock again. One minute. "Linnea? I'm going to have to go in a sec."

"Okay, wait. This is why I called. You said he wasn't your boyfriend but..."

"He's not."

"Okay. It's just, I think he might not have been totally honest with you. Eric says he didn't drop out, he got kicked out."

"Kicked out?"

"Yeah. For assaulting a teacher."

I hold my breath. "Mr. Lawson?"

"I don't know. Eric said it was just a rumor; he didn't see it or anything. I guess no one saw it."

He'd told me Mr. Lawson had assaulted him. Shoved him up against the lockers. I remembered the look in his eyes when he talked about it. *It was his word against mine. You can guess who the principal believed.* I believed Leo. Maybe he had pushed Mr. Lawson away, or even struck out at him, but I had no trouble believing that Mr. Lawson had started it.

Still…If anyone had reason to hate GRSS, Leo certainly did.

I sit in my room and stare at my half-written essay. If I'd had doubts about whether Leo would really go along with Jamie's plan, they're gone now. Jamie's angry all the time, but his anger is obvious: blazing flashes of heat and flame, all on the surface. Leo's is hidden and carefully controlled, but from what Linnea told me, I'm guessing it's been smoldering for years. And Jamie's been fanning the embers.

I shiver and put my pen down. There doesn't seem much point in finishing my paper if the school isn't even going to be there in the morning.

At some point I hear Dad come back from wherever he's been, and a little while later, Mom calls me for dinner. I ignore her. I'm not hungry and I don't feel like talking.

Eventually it starts to get dark. I can't stop thinking about Parker. I keep picturing her at the social skills group, laughing and eating rose petals, that wide smile on her thin face. So beautiful in her own way. Then I remember how she looked standing there at school, all blotchy-faced and unhappy. I imagine her getting caught at the school, being hauled down to the police station and charged with arson. They won't care that it wasn't her idea or that she didn't want to be there. They won't care that she didn't feel like she had a choice.

I finally come up with a plan. It is a bit of a lousy plan—there are about a thousand things that could go wrong—but given that I am grounded and basically a prisoner, it's the best I can do.

I go downstairs and chat with my parents for a few minutes, like nothing is wrong. I heap dinner leftovers—a mess of lentils and undercooked brown rice—onto a plate. I'm suddenly starving. I pretty much inhale it without even bothering to heat it up first. Then I say good night to my parents, head back upstairs, brush my teeth, lie down on my bed and wait.

EIGHTEEN

At ten thirty, the stairs creak as Mom and Dad head up to their room. At eleven, I slip out of bed, peer down the hall to check if their light is off and listen for a few minutes. Silence.

I pull on my jacket and pad as quietly as I can down the dark stairway. They're both sound sleepers, but I don't even want to think about how much trouble I'll be in if I get caught.

I tiptoe across the huge front hall with its high ceiling and cool tiled floor; then I slip my feet into my runners and open the front door without a sound. I guess that's one good thing about a new house. Our old place had squeaky floorboards and a front door that creaked so loudly it could probably wake the neighbors.

Outside, rain is falling softly and so slowly it appears to hang in the air, suspended; it is almost a mist. No one is around. Across the street, one light is on in an upstairs bedroom. Next door you can see the bluish glow of a TV through the half-open blinds. I walk down the driveway, hoping no one will look out the window and report back to my parents tomorrow. I stop at the end of the drive and stand there for a moment, staring at the glowing bowlingball lamps like they are crystal balls that can tell me something useful. They glow blankly back.

I guess this is my last chance to change my mind and sneak back inside. But then I think about Parker—how scared she sounded and how hopeless—and I'm pretty sure I'm doing the right thing, even if my parents wouldn't think so.

I have to talk to her.

Of course, her place is downtown, maybe fifteen kilometers away, and when you're stuck out in the burbs you can't just hop on a bus. The thought of taking my parents' car crosses my mind, but only briefly. I'm pretty sure I wouldn't even be able to get it out of the garage without waking them. Besides, even though I have a basic understanding of how to drive, I haven't actually got my license yet.

I look at my watch—five past eleven—and start to run. I have to get to Parker's place before Leo does. Before it is too late.

By the time I finally get out to the main road, it's pouring. My heart is pounding, my shirt is soaked with sweat, and the rain has plastered my hair to my head. Eleven fifteen. I start to jog backward down the side of the road, holding out one hand. Thumb up. I hope I won't get picked up by some pervert. Or, more likely and almost as scary, one of my parents' friends.

Cars zip past, spraying me with sheets of dirty water.

I keep moving and dripping and doing my best not to think about Jamie hitting Parker, or about my parents, or about the school burning down. Eventually, a car stops.

"Where you headed?" a girl yells out the window. She is maybe two or three years older than me, with straight red hair and orthodontist-perfect teeth.

"Downtown. King and James area."

She nods and gestures to the back door. "Hop in."

I slump into the backseat and try to catch my breath. Eleven twenty-five. It shouldn't take more than ten minutes to get there. Now if only I can get Parker alone.

The girl who picked me up introduces herself as Alice and tells me she's meeting her boyfriend, who's a musician, at a downtown bar. I don't feel like chatting, so I just nod a lot and make interested noises and tell her I'm going to visit a friend. By the time we pull up at the corner of King and James, the rain has mostly stopped. I nod thanks to Alice and hurry down the street toward Parker's place. The pizza joint downstairs is practically empty. I take the stairs two at a time, praying that it will be Parker and not Jamie who answers the door. If it's Jamie, I'm pretty sure there's no hope at all.

But it's Parker. She has her jacket and boots on, like she is about to go out. The bruise is still there, a yellow-green smudge under her eye, but when she sees me she grins widely and she looks like the old, happy Parker.

"Who is it? Is it Leo?" Jamie calls out.

I grab her arm and pull her outside. "Come on. I need to talk to you."

Parker resists for a second; then she steps out into the hall. "Just a sec," she calls back to Jamie.

I close the door. "Come on."

"I can't," Parker says. "Leo's going to be here any moment." But she follows me down the stairs anyway.

I look at my watch. Eleven forty. "Not for twenty minutes," I say. "Just walk around the block with me."

Outside, Parker takes a deep breath and lets out a long shaky sigh. "Look, I know what you're going to say. I know this is stupid."

"So don't go along with it then."

She doesn't say anything. She starts walking quickly down the empty sidewalk.

"Parker...I'm not crazy about school, you know that. But I don't see the point of doing this. It's not going to change anything."

"I know, I know. You don't have to persuade me."

I hesitate. "You said something once about maybe going back to school. Then you said, 'Don't tell Jamie.'"

I try to meet her eyes but she is walking so fast that I practically have to jog to keep up. "What's going on?"

She shakes her head. "It's complicated."

"You told me I had choices, okay? You helped me to see that." I grab her wrist. "Parker. Stop."

She stops walking and turns to face me. Her eyes are wet.

"You've got choices too," I tell her. "You do."

She is silent. I'm still holding her wrist, almost holding her hand, and she doesn't pull away. We stand there under a streetlight, in the slow cold drizzle, cars driving past. Water trickles down my face. Someone honks their horn as they drive by. Neon lights flash red, green, blue in the darkness. I feel like time is standing still.

"It's easy to talk about making choices," Parker says at last. "But they have a way of biting you on the ass."

"What do you mean?"

"You make one choice, and then all of a sudden you don't have the same choices you used to have. You think I like my life right now?"

Then Parker looks up at me with those pale eyes, and something flips and tumbles inside my chest. My heart is doing something crazy, falling from its precarious perch. I let go of her wrist and step back. "I don't know. Don't you?"

"It's not like I enjoy flipping pancakes at the Golden Griddle," she says. "I have to pay the rent. God knows Jamie won't." She starts to cry silently, big tears rolling slowly down her cheeks.

I put my arms around her and sneak a peek at my watch over her shoulder. Eleven forty-five. "Parker...you can't stay with someone who hits you."

She cries harder, her whole body shaking.

I can feel the sharp edges of her shoulder blades beneath my hands. I close my eyes and wonder what she'd say if I told her I was falling for her, what she would do if she knew how I felt. Whether she'd push me away.

"He used to be different," she says. She lifts her head from my shoulder and looks up at me again, and again my heart starts to go crazy.

Under the streetlight, I can see that her face is wet with tears, but she doesn't wipe them away.

"He hasn't had an easy time," she says. "His family..."

"Oh please." I'm suddenly furious and I'm not sure whether it's her or Jamie or myself that I'm angry with. "Give me a fucking break."

For a moment I think she is going to get mad. Then she suddenly laughs. A bitter laugh, but a laugh all the same.

"You're right," she admits. "But...what else would I do?"

"Whatever you want."

We stare at each other in silence for a moment.

"Look at you," she says. "You're soaked."

"I'm okay. Parker..."

"I can't go back to my parents," she says softly.

"What happened? I mean, did they...did they hurt you or something?"

"Not physically. Nothing like that. They just fought all the time. Yelling at each other, throwing things, slamming doors. And it was always about me, always my fault." She shakes her head. "They had...they had all these crazy rules, like I had to be home by eight o'clock. I mean, eight o'clock? I couldn't even do band at school because the concerts went later than that. The only remotely social thing I could go to was a Bible study group."

"Wow. I thought my parents were strict."

"That's just an example. I could go on and on. My dad's ex-military, and I swear, it was like boot camp or something. He'd decide what I could wear, who I could see, where I could go. I couldn't deal with it, you know?"

"No kidding. Who could?"

She gives me a small, crooked smile. "Well, I started seeing someone and they found out and freaked completely. Wouldn't let me go anywhere, drove me to and from school...I kind of lost it. I started running away and not coming home for days at a time. And I was doing a lot of drugs, Ecstasy and stuff, getting all screwed up."

I remember something she'd said before, about Jamie. "You said Jamie sort of saved your life. Is that what you meant?"

"Yeah. I was acting kind of crazy, and my dad was totally losing it and taking me to all these shrinks, trying to get me locked up or something."

"I don't think they usually lock people up. Not kids anyway."

She shrugs. "He'd have liked them to give me a lobotomy, I guess. But they just kept me overnight and then prescribed a bunch of meds that I refused to take. So we all ended up in family counseling, which was a nightmare because anything I said my parents would twist around and use against me, but the one good thing was that the counselor persuaded my parents to let me get a job."

"The Golden Griddle?"

"Yeah. And then I met Jamie and moved in with him pretty much right away." She grins. "Which I guess confirmed all my parents' fears about letting me work."

"Wow. I guess so."

She lifts her chin and looks up at me. "Jamie really did help me though. I stopped using drugs and everything."

Parker's never said much about herself before, and I don't want her to stop talking, but I'm starting to get nervous about Leo showing up and seeing us. "That's great. I mean, I'm glad you moved out then. But now what, Parker? You can't go along with this business of burning down the school."

"I know. But you heard Jamie this afternoon. He's all, 'If you're not with us, you're against us.'"

"Yeah. I know. But you don't need them. You could get your own place. It's not like Jamie's helping you out any, with money, I mean." I hesitate. "You could even go back to school, if you wanted to."

"It wouldn't be that easy."

"You could do it though." I shove my cold hands into my jacket pockets. "We'd figure it out, Parker. We would."

A small smile slowly lifts the corners of her mouth. "We? You and me?"

I'm not sure what I'm agreeing to, but I don't care.

"Yeah. You and me." I meet her eyes, and my heart skips a beat. She has absolutely no idea how I feel. She has a boyfriend, I remind myself. She's straight, straight, straight. Forget it, Dante. Don't be stupid.

Parker wipes the tears from her cheeks with the palms of her hands. "Okay," she whispers. She lets out a long shaky sigh and looks back down the sidewalk toward her place. "So...what do we do now?"

I swallow hard. "Let's get out of here," I say. "Let's go somewhere. Boston, maybe. Or New York."

NINETEEN

I don't think I expected Parker to agree. I just threw it out there: a crazy idea, an impulse. New York.

But Parker jumps on it. "Hell, yeah," she says. She brushes the backs of her hands across her eyes, wiping tears away. "Let's go. My car's in front of the apartment."

"Got your keys?"

She checks her jacket pockets. "Yeah. Lucky."

We start walking and we're almost there when I see a station wagon pull over and park across the street. I grab Parker's arm. "Is that Leo?"

"Crap." She opens the door to the pizza place and pulls me inside. "Do you think he saw us?"

"I don't know."

We stand there under the bright lights, surrounded by the laughter and loud voices of mostly drunk customers, the sign in the window flashing *2 for 1 "slices"* in backward writing, mirror writing. Leo gets out of his car and heads toward us.

"Crap," Parker says again.

I can't think what to do.

"Can I help you girls?" the man behind the counter asks impatiently. "Or were you planning just to stand there admiring the view?"

I spin around. "Yes! Um, two slices of pepperoni and pineapple."

Parker looks at me like I've lost it. "You're not seriously thinking about food right now?"

I smile tightly. "Play along, okay?"

There is a cool draft as the door opens, and I turn around. "Hey! Leo."

He tilts his head quizzically. "Dante? What are you doing here?"

"Lawson was such an ass this afternoon," I say. "I decided you were right. Screw it. I'm in." I raise one eyebrow. "If it's not too late?"

"You're in?" He grins. "I figured you just got nervous earlier. We shouldn't have sprung it on you like that."

I feel a pang of guilt, lying to him. Part of me wants to trust him, give him a chance, try and talk him out of doing this. But I can't risk it. "Tell Jamie we'll be up in a minute. You want anything?"

"Nah. See you upstairs." He heads back out, and the guy behind the counter slides two hot greasy slices toward me. I take my time finding my money, giving Leo time to get up the stairs.

Beside me, Parker is in a fit of giggles. "Oh god, oh god. You were so cool. He had no idea."

I hand her a slice of pizza. "Eat up. It's a long way to New York."

She starts laughing harder. "We're going? We're really going?"

"We're really going," I say.

Two minutes later, we are in her car, pulling away from the curb and laughing hysterically.

"I don't have any of my stuff," Parker says. "Any clothes or anything. I can't believe we're doing this."

I check my wallet. I have thirty-five bucks. "Um, Parker? How much gas do we have?"

"Full tank." Parker turns on the radio. "And my money's under the seat. If I leave it in the apartment, Jamie spends it."

"Yeah? How much?"

"Not much. Ten bucks, maybe."

I turn up the heat, shivering in my damp clothes. Forty-five bucks isn't going to get us all the way to New York, but I figure we can sort out those details along the way. The windshield wipers slap back and forth and the Plain White T's are on the radio, singing, "Hey there, Delilah." Parker turns it up, and I laugh, singing along: "'What's it like in New York City...'"

"It's a sign, Parker," I say. "An omen. You know, I've always wanted to go to New York. We could ride the subway and go to Times Square and..."

"We could do anything," Parker says. "We could do anything we want." She turns onto the highway. The digital clock on the dashboard reads twelve o'clock.

We made it, I think. We got away. I roll down my window, stick my face out into the rain and let out a loud whoop. I can hear Parker's laugh, the music on the radio, the sound of the tires racing along the wet road. We're leaving it all behind: my parents, Mr. Lawson, Jamie and Leo, the burning school.

Not our problem anymore.

We are heading out of town when Parker says, "You think we should call? I mean, the guys might think, I don't know. That something happened to us."

"What, like we got kidnapped by the pizza shop guy?" I still feel giddy and light-headed, on the edge of laughter.

"Yeah." She giggles; then she turns serious. "They'll worry. You know they will."

"Whatever. Too bad for them." But I wish she hadn't said it. I'm crashing back down to earth, the euphoria suddenly gone. I bite my lip, thinking. I'm going to have to call my parents. They'll be wrecks if they get up in the morning and I'm not there.

Parker looks sideways at me. She has an odd expression on her face—sort of challenging but curious too. "Leo really likes you, you know. He told me."

"I like him too. Just not that way."

"He's such a good guy though. And he's cute, don't you think?"

"Yeah, well. I guess I just don't want to get involved with anyone right now." It's such a lie. I'd get involved with Parker in a second, given the chance.

"Probably a good call." Parker sighs. "I feel so confused about everything. I don't know how it all got so messed up." She drums her fingers on the steering wheel. "I still think schools are basically prisons."

"Sure they are," I say. I remember the first time I saw her, and I laugh. "Woof, woof. You are not a dog…"

She laughs too, but there is something sad about it. "It's all over, isn't it? Our group. All of that."

I think for a minute. "It doesn't have to be," I say at last. "But…well, you're done with Jamie, right?"

She nods, but her eyes slide away from mine. My heart sinks. *I love you, Parker.* I let myself imagine, just for a second, saying the words out loud. I wonder what she'd do. Get all freaked out, maybe, or pretend she thinks I mean I only love her as a friend. I close my eyes and lean my hot cheek against the cool glass of the window. It doesn't make the slightest bit of difference how I feel, because she's never going to feel the same way about me.

There's a long pause and then Parker says, "What do you mean, it doesn't have to be over?"

She is watching the road, eyes straight ahead, lips slightly parted. Her face, in profile, is so perfect. I clench my fists and try to drag my thoughts back to the conversation. The one that is actually happening, not the crazy one in my head. "Well…you and I can do what we want, right? I mean, we could keep doing the kind of thing you were doing. Flyers, you know. And talking to people."

"I guess so." Her voice is flat.

"I know it'd be different, without the others. But it might be better, even."

She glances at me. "Better how?"

"Well…It seemed like we were always against everything, you know? Anti-compulsory education, anti-war, anti-this, anti-that."

"So? What choice is there? I mean, we're not going to be pro-war, or—"

I cut her off. "I know, I'm not explaining myself well. I just thought…well, maybe we could think about what we stand *for*, you know? Like, being for peace instead of against war."

"It's the same thing. It's just different words."

I suddenly feel tired and sort of depressed. "Maybe."

We drive in silence for a few minutes. Something has shifted, and I'm not sure why, but the feeling of excitement has gone. Parker's face is pale and the shadows under her eyes look like bruises. The thought slides into my head, unwanted and unwelcome: *She's going to go back to Jamie.* Despite everything, she's going to go back to him. I open my mouth to ask her but then I stop myself—if she isn't thinking about him, I don't want to bring up the subject. "You okay, Parker?" I say instead.

Parker doesn't answer right away, but she eases up on the gas pedal and the car slows. Then she sighs. "Not really."

I look away from her and stare at the road ahead. I know she's thinking about him. My chest is all tight and I try to catch my breath, but it's like my lungs won't inflate fully.

"We shouldn't have taken off," she says. "We should've tried to talk them out of it. If they go ahead…I know it's stupid, but I don't want to see Jamie get in trouble, you know?"

Oh, Parker. Without even being here, Jamie is reeling her back in. I don't care if he gets caught—I don't give a shit what happens to him. Still, Parker's got me thinking about the guys now, and I can't help feeling worried about Leo. I wish I'd tried to talk to him back in the pizza place. He might have listened. "Maybe all the rain…you know, maybe the school will be too wet to burn?"

"Maybe. And maybe the school will be a pile of ash by the morning. What do we know about starting fires, Dante?"

I imagine everyone arriving in the morning and seeing the school all burned and roped off. Or maybe they'll hear about it on the radio over breakfast or see it on TV. I imagine Mrs. Greenway and wonder if she'd think I had something to do with it. I hope she'd know I wouldn't do that, but I'm not sure. "Shit," I say. "This is so messed up. I mean, some people are going to be really upset. Devastated."

"Well, yeah. I guess some people like school."

"Yeah, and some don't, but they don't want to flip pancakes forever either."

Parker frowns. "Yeah, ha fucking ha. So what's your point?"

I'm not sure exactly what my point is but I know something is totally messed up about all this. "So…what if I *don't* want to drop out? What if I want to keep going to GRSS?"

"Do you?"

I have no idea what I want right now. Except Parker. I'm pretty sure I want Parker. "I don't know. But that should be my choice, right? Isn't that the whole point?"

Parker turns off the radio. The windshield wipers slap back and forth, back and forth. "Yeah," she says, "I guess."

I think of the line from the *Divine Comedy* that I loved so much. "You know what Dante said? He said 'If the present world go astray, the cause is in you, in you it is to be sought.'"

She nods. "I looked up Dante online, after you told me about the circles of hell and all that. He said something else I liked too: 'The hottest places in hell are reserved for those who, in time of great moral crisis, maintain their neutrality.'"

I look at her, startled. That quote was what made me want to read the *Inferno* in the first place, but I read the whole thing, cover to cover, and that line wasn't there. In fact, the souls of people who never took a stand were sort of on the outskirts of hell, not in the hottest places at all. So I googled it and guess what? Turns out someone famous—JFK, I think—quoted that line as Dante, and it sort of stuck. I've even seen it on bumper stickers.

Dante Alighieri is most famous for a line he never even wrote. "Yeah," I say, sighing, "I love that line too."

Neither of us says anything for a couple of minutes, but I know it's over. We're not running away together. We're not going to New York.

Parker turns to me. "We have to go back, don't we."

It isn't a question. I nod. "Yeah," I say. "We have to go back."

TWENTY

I half expect to see smoke when we pull up at the school, but I can't see anything unusual. No Jamie, no Leo, no fire.

"Where are they?" Parker whispers. "You think they're still waiting for us? Or looking for us?"

I open my mouth to answer; then I spot Leo's car, parked at the far end of the lot where it backs onto the sports field. "They're here," I say, pointing. "They're really going to do it."

"I bet they'll light the fire around the back," Parker says. "That's what they were planning anyway."

We run along the side of the school, past the long wall of the gymnasium and around the corner. It all feels unreal to me. I still can't quite believe they would actually try to burn the school down.

Then I see them. Leo and Jamie, right by the school wall. Right outside Mr. Lawson's classroom window. Jamie is holding a red jerry can in one hand. I stop running and stand motionless for a second, immobilized by shock. They're doing it. They're really doing it. With sudden despair, I realize we've miscalculated. They're not going to listen to us. We shouldn't even be here.

"Gas," Parker breathes.

"Hey!" I shout.

Leo and Jamie freeze. Then they spot us.

"Christ," Jamie says, "I thought you guys were the cops." He grins at Parker. "I knew you'd change your mind."

"We haven't changed our minds," Parker says. She looks at Leo, not Jamie. "We came back to try to…well, to ask you not to do it."

Jamie snorts. "Go home, Parker. If you're not helping us, then get out of the way."

"Just listen for a minute," I plead. "I'm all about doing things that make people think. But this won't." I look at Leo. "The first time I met you, you said we have more choices than we think, right?"

He nods. "So?"

I gesture at the school. "I know you had some bad times here, okay? I know about what happened to you here."

His mouth twists. "You don't know shit, Dante."

"I believe you, Leo. About Mr. Lawson. And I don't blame you for being angry. But—"

He cuts me off. "This isn't about me."

"Yeah? You sure about that?" I lift my chin and meet his gaze full-on. "Fine then. It's not about you. But it's about me, isn't it?" I raise my voice. "What if I want to keep going to school?"

Leo frowns. "It's not about you either, Dante. It's about taking a stand."

Parker steps closer to me. "That's what Dante and I are doing, Leo. Taking a stand."

There was a long silence. Leo nods his head slowly, like he's willing to listen to her. For a second I think we've won.

Then Jamie laughs, a cold mean laugh that tells me we haven't won at all. "Stupid bitch," he says to Parker. "You and your stupid dyke friend."

He pulls his hand from his pocket and tosses something onto the gas-soaked ground.

There is a roar and a flash. A sheet of flame shoots up the side of the building. I just stand there for a moment, staring. The building is lit up, the gray of its walls glowing a weird pale orange. It looks massive and solid, and I wonder if it will really burn. It's brick, after all. I find myself hoping that maybe, despite how awful it looks, they won't be able to do too much damage.

Parker starts to cry. "Please don't do this. Please stop."

Leo looks at her; then he turns to Jamie. "Jamie, let's go. You've made your point, right? Let's get out of here."

Jamie shakes his head. "Fuck, no. Don't wuss out on me now. We haven't even started."

Leo hesitates. I can see the indecision flickering across his face. It's up to him. If he's staying with Jamie—if he wants to be a part of this—there's nothing I can do.

Except get the hell out of here and take Parker with me. I grab her arm. "Parker, come on. Let's go."

Parker looks back at Jamie, her faced streaked with tears. "Jamie? Don't be mad."

"Fuck, Parker. I don't have time for your drama, okay? If you want to go, just go. You too, Leo. You're as bad as the girls. No wonder everyone called you a fag."

"Fuck you," Leo says softly.

I tug on Parker's arm, but she just stands there, still crying. Her face is lit up by the orange glow of the flames, and weirdly, I notice that she has eyebrow stubble. We're going to get caught, I think, and my chest clutches tight with fear. I dig my fingers into her arm, hard. "Parker. Come *on*."

"I'm going with Dante," she tells Jamie. "Okay?"

Jamie doesn't say anything, but his face is twisted with rage. He picks up a large rock from the ground and hurls it toward a first-floor window. Mr. Lawson's classroom. There is a crash and a shower of broken glass falls onto the ground.

"Don't," I say, hopelessly.

He laughs, a cold hard laugh, and pulls a bottle from his backpack. I blink. I can't think what it is for a second. Then I notice the rag sticking out the top.

"Jamie...wait a minute. Please don't..."

Jamie ignores me. He grabs the jerry can and pours gas on the rag. "This is for you, Dante. Watch it burn." He laughs again and flicks open his lighter. "Dante's fucking inferno."

"Don't, Jamie." Leo moves to grab his arm, but not fast enough. Jamie lights the rag and in one smooth motion, tosses the bottle through the broken window.

There is a second's silence.

Then an explosion. Flames shoot out the window and a blast of heat pushes me back.

"Shit. *Shit.*" Leo takes a few steps back; then he turns and starts to run across the field.

Parker clutches my arm. "Come on."

I can't move. I just stand there, staring, barely able to breathe.

"Dante! Come on." She tugs on my arm again.

I turn toward her and I realize I'm crying, tears stinging my eyes and blurring everything into an orange haze.

"We have to get out of here," she says. "Now."

We start running and we don't stop until we reach her car.

Parker drives fast, tires screeching as she pulls out of the parking lot and heads for the main road. Behind us, I can see the glow of the fire.

"Now what?" Parker asks.

My heart is pounding so hard I think I might throw up. "Where's Leo?"

"I don't know."

I squint into the darkness, but I can't see him. "He was ahead of us."

"Should we look for him? I mean, I don't want to just..."

"We should get the hell out of here," I say. "Like, right now."

Parker barely pauses at a stop sign, and I grab her arm. "Drive normal, for god's sake. Don't act like this is some getaway car."

She nods and slows down. "Are you thinking what I'm thinking?"

"Calling the fire department?"

She nods. "Yeah. I don't mean to rat him out or anything..."

"We don't have to give names."

I pull out my cell phone, and Parker grabs my arm to stop me. "Isn't that, like, traceable?" She gestures to a gas station up ahead. "Look. Pay phone."

I sigh. I am absolutely the last person I ever thought would try to save my school. "Okay. Let's do it."

Parker pulls into the gas station and we both get out of the car. She dials; then she passes me the phone.

My hand is shaking as I take the receiver from her. "I'm calling to report a fire," I tell the operator. "At Glen Ridge Secondary School."

"Now what?" Parker asks as we drive away from the gas station. She looks at me, then back at the road. "I guess we're not really going to New York."

I think about it. Somehow it no longer feels like such a great idea. We've got no money, and I guess it'd just be running away from everything. It wouldn't be my real life. Anyway, it'd kill my parents. "I don't know," I say. "Maybe not tonight anyway."

She sighs. "I know. Well, it was a fun idea while it lasted."

The clock on the dash flashes *2:25*. "What next then? I mean, where are you going to go?"

"Home, I guess."

"To Jamie."

"What else am I going to do?"

There's a catch in her voice that makes me want to put my arms around her. I want to fix everything, to take care of her, make her happy. Maybe if I told her how much I care about her...*Bad, bad idea.* I ball up my hands into tight fists and press them against my thighs. "Do you have enough money to get your own place?"

She gives a short bitter laugh. "Are you kidding?"

There is a short silence. I don't know what to suggest. I guess there must be people who could help, like social workers or something, but I don't really have a clue about that. "Um, what about your counselor? Could you call her?"

"I'll call her tomorrow." She leans back against the headrest and closes her eyes. "But what can she do? I mean, she'll be supportive and everything, and maybe she'd try to persuade my folks to let me move back in for a while, but I don't want to do that. I don't want to go to some group home either, which is what she thinks I should do."

I feel like someone should be able to help, but I guess no one is going to hand her the thousand bucks she'd need for first and last months' rent. "Um, do you want to come to my place? Like, just for tonight, anyway?"

She opens her eyes and turns toward me. "Wouldn't your parents freak? I mean, they don't even know you're out."

"Mm. I'm supposed to be grounded." Mom would have a hard time putting a positive spin on my arriving home in the middle of the night with a strange girl with no eyebrows. Almost no eyebrows. On the other hand, I can't think of anywhere else to go, and the trouble I'd get into seems insignificant beside the idea of Parker having to go back to Jamie. "Did you know your eyebrows are growing back?" I ask her.

She nods. "So is your hair."

I run my hand over my head. Still fuzz. "So, what happened? I mean, how come you shaved them off?"

Parker shrugs. "Bad day, I guess. I didn't shave them though. I was actually just tweezing out a few hairs, only for some reason I couldn't stop."

I nod, like it makes perfect sense to completely remove your eyebrows.

She looks at me, makes a face and starts to laugh. I can't help laughing too. It's just the stress of the night, I guess, but soon I'm losing it, laughing too hard, laughing as if something's really funny when really everything is kind of a mess. Parker is totally cracking up too, rocking slightly in her seat. I watch her—her thin face lit up with laughter, her eyes narrowed to slits, her cheeks flushed.

I take a deep breath and look out in to the darkness of the empty parking lot. *God, I am so crazy about her.*

Parker suddenly stops laughing and holds up one hand. "Can you hear that?"

Far away, sirens are wailing faintly. Jamie will hear them, I think. He'll be long gone by the time the fire trucks arrive. "You think they'll be able to save the school?"

She taps her spidery fingers on the steering wheel. "I don't know. I mean, I don't think it'll have burned to the ground yet or anything, but there's gotta be a lot of damage." She looks at me sideways. "It's not going to be open for business as usual tomorrow."

"I guess not." I wonder, again, if Mrs. Greenway will suspect me of being involved. I hope not. If she asks, I'll tell her the truth. I'll tell her that I didn't know for sure it would happen and that I tried to stop it. I know what Leo would say—that teachers never believe students. But I am pretty sure Mrs. G. would believe me. Leo doesn't know everything. "You think we should've done more? I mean, like called the cops or something, before they actually started the fire?"

"I don't know. I've been thinking that too." She watches the road ahead. "I guess maybe we should have, but I couldn't have done it, you know? I couldn't get them into that kind of trouble."

I don't say anything right away. It makes me angry that I have to share the responsibility for this, at least a little bit. *If the present world go astray...* Well, it definitely did that. I let out a long sigh. "You know, on some level, I guess

I didn't believe they'd go through with it. Not so seriously, you know? Not such a big fire." It sounds stupid. Like what, I thought maybe they were going to have a campfire? Toss a match in a garbage can? I close my eyes for a second. All I see is flickering flames. I can still feel the scorching blast of heat on my face and hear Jamie's taunting laugh, his voice. *Dante's fucking inferno.* A knot of guilt twists inside my stomach. "How come Jamie hates me so much?" I ask.

She doesn't answer right away. I shift in my seat, turning sideways to face her. "Parker? Do you know why? I mean, it's not just tonight. He hasn't liked me from the start."

"He's an asshole."

"Duh." I force a grin, trying to lighten the mood.

She looks uncomfortable. "It doesn't matter what he thinks."

I know the answer anyway. *Your stupid dyke friend,* Jamie had said. What I can't figure out is why he said it. He can't possibly know about Beth. I guess I am queer or bi or whatever, but there's no way he could know that. He doesn't know anything about me. "He thinks I'm queer. Is that it?"

Parker slows down as she passes a highway turnoff. "Where are we going? My mind is so not on the road; I totally shouldn't be driving."

"Pull over," I say. "Until we figure out where to go."

"Yeah. Okay." A McDonald's is on the next block, and she pulls into the empty parking lot and switches the engine off.

It is suddenly very quiet. I figure Parker changed the subject on purpose. Obviously just the idea that Jamie thinks

I might be queer makes her uncomfortable. My throat
starts to feel all tight and achy. I wish I hadn't brought it
up. I think about Linnea and her queer students group.
I'm not a joiner, but maybe I should check it out, or at
least talk to Linnea. It'd be a relief to talk about some
of this stuff with someone who isn't freaked out by the
whole subject.

Parker rolls down her window and lights a cigarette.
"Sorry. I know smoking in cars is kind of gross."

"It's your car." I wish she didn't smoke at all. I don't
mind the smell, but I hate what she's doing to her lungs.
She'd make a good runner too, with her light build and
those long legs. "Listen, I know what Jamie thinks and I
don't care. It doesn't matter. Forget I asked."

"No, it's okay. He just says stuff without thinking sometimes, you know?"

I hope she's not going to give me more reasons why
Jamie isn't all that bad. Or, even worse, try to reassure me
that she knows I'm not a dyke.

"He's just possessive. He doesn't like it when I have
friends, that's all. I mean, he doesn't even like me seeing
Leo when he's not around. He doesn't really think, you
know, that you're…"

She can't even say the word. I have to tell her though.
I mean, if I don't say something now, I'm basically lying to
her. I try to take a deep breath but I feel like there's a giant
hand pushing down on my chest. "Parker," I say.

She takes a drag on her cigarette and turns away to
blow the smoke out the window. "You know, it's just what

he says when he's pissed off at someone. Like calling Leo a fag. He knows that's not true either."

"Parker." I'm running through possible ways of saying this inside my head. *Parker, it's no big deal, but Jamie's not exactly wrong.* But this isn't about Jamie. It's about being honest with Parker. *Um, Parker? I don't want to have secrets from you.* Or maybe, *Parker, I guess I should tell you something.* I can't get any of the words past my throat. I'm as bad as Beth. I'm chicken-shit.

Parker is sort of staring at me, and I have to say something. But I can't do it. I can't tell her.

"What?" she says. "What's wrong?"

"Look...," I say. "I think you should come home with me."

Her non-eyebrows lift.

I clear my throat. "I mean, it's none of my business, but I'm kind of worried about you going home tonight. Jamie seemed pretty pissed off."

"I know. But if I'm not there..." She shrugs. "He'll be more pissed off tomorrow."

"I thought you told me earlier that you were done with him." I feel suddenly, unreasonably, angry. "All that stuff about maybe going back to school, getting your own place. I guess that was all bullshit, huh?"

I regret the words the second they leave my mouth. Parker looks at me wide-eyed, a puppy that just got kicked. She butts out her cigarette in the car's ashtray, rolls up her window and wraps her arms around herself. "I know," she whispers. "It wasn't bullshit. I meant it.

I just…it's hard, Dante. I love him. You know? I mean, I know he's not always…you know, he does stuff sometimes…but…"

My anger is gone like it never existed. I can't fit this Parker together with the tough beautiful girl eating rose petals at Shelley's group. She's getting sucked right back in to the same shit, throwing her life away for some jerk who doesn't deserve her. *Oh, Parker*, I think. *Please, please don't go back to him.* "You want to stay with me for a couple days? Until you figure it out?" I ask her again. "I mean, Mom might freak a little, but I'm already grounded anyway."

"You really think your folks would let me stay?"

"Oh yeah. For a few days anyway." No matter how mad my mother is at me, she won't turn Parker out if she has nowhere else to go. More likely, she'll send me to my room and treat Parker like an orphaned kitten.

She hesitates; then she nods. "Okay. Okay. For tonight, maybe. Thanks, Dante." A frown crosses her face. "The fire will be on the news tomorrow. If they know you were out, will they suspect you were involved?"

"Not a chance," I say. "Not in a million years."

"We can both sneak in," she suggests. "They don't even need to know you were out at all. In the morning, I'll tell them I had nowhere to go so I came over. They shouldn't get too upset with you over that."

I breathe a sigh of relief. "Parker, you are a genius. Why didn't I think of that?"

"Oh, I don't know. Less practice at lying to your folks than me, maybe?"

I've lied to mine more in the past two weeks than I have in my whole life. I feel a twinge of guilt, but I push it aside. Telling the truth isn't an option. It isn't even imaginable.

It's well past three by the time we pull into the maze of streets I call home. Parker pulls over at the end of my street, turns the engine and lights off and coasts to a stop a few houses away from mine. She looks at me. "Ready?"

"Ready."

We walk up my driveway, and I unlock the front door as slowly and quietly as I can. "Okay, follow me." I cross the front hall and head upstairs, barely breathing. Behind me, Parker's footsteps are as light as an elf's. At the top of the hall, I turn and beckon to her. It's pitch dark; I don't think she can even see me. "This way," I whisper. "Come on."

She grabs my arm and I lead her down the hall. I'm just opening my door when ahead of us, at the far end of the hall, a crack of light appears under my parents' bedroom door. I freeze and Parker's fingertips dig into the back of my arm.

The door opens, spilling light into the hallway. Mom steps out. "Dante? Are you up? I thought I heard…" She sees Parker and stops abruptly. "What's going on?"

I wonder if there is any possibility that she won't notice we're both fully dressed. As in, jackets and all. As in, we've been out all night. "Uhh…Mom, this is Parker. She kind of needs a place to stay for a few days."

Mom ignores Parker. She stares at me like I've completely lost it. "You've been out, haven't you? Emily, tell me you didn't sneak out after we were in bed."

"Um. Well."

"I can't believe this." She raises her voice, and a second later I hear Dad stomping around in the bedroom.

He pokes his head and his naked hairy shoulders out into the hall. "Oops. Just a minute." He disappears again, obviously looking for clothes to put on.

"Where have you been?" Mom steps closer to us and frowns. "You smell like smoke."

Crap. Crap crap crap. I look at Parker and she stares back at me, wide-eyed. I don't know what to do. The thing is, I want to tell the truth. Partly because I hate lying to my parents, but also because I really don't feel like I've done anything wrong. I had to sneak out to try to help Parker. I had to try to stop Jamie and Leo. I'd do the same thing again, if I had to do it over. But if I tell the truth, I know my parents will insist that we go to the police. And even though I think what Jamie did is wrong, even though I worry about what else he might do, I still don't want to turn him in for it.

TWENTY-ONE

Five minutes later we are all sitting down around the kitchen table to "talk about this in a civilized manner." Mom's words. She is wrapped in a silk housecoat and her face is shiny with anti-aging night lotion. Dad, to my relief, is fully dressed in sweats and a T-shirt. Parker sticks close to my side and keeps muttering that she's sorry and that this is all her fault. I'm not sure if she's talking to me or to my parents.

Mom looks at us both, eyes steely. "I'd like an explanation from you, Dante."

"It's kind of complicated," I say. Stalling, trying to decide how much to tell them.

She just waits.

"It's my fault," Parker says. "I didn't have anywhere to go. I'm sorry. Dante was only trying to help me out."

"Thank you," my mother says, "but I'd like to hear from my daughter."

Parker nods and stares at the table. Dad gives her a small encouraging smile, but she misses it.

"Mom. Um, okay. You know when Parker called earlier tonight and you made me get off the phone? And I said she was crying?"

She nods.

"Well, she didn't call back and she doesn't have a phone so I couldn't call her. But I was worried about her."

Mom looks disbelieving. "That hardly justifies lying to us and sneaking out of the house after we're in bed. We thought we could trust you, Emily. Now I don't know what to think. Are you..." She lowers her voice. "Are you using drugs? Is that it?"

I shake my head impatiently. "No. Of course not." My hands are sweating, and I wipe them on my jeans, under the table. I look at my dad. His heavy eyebrows are lowered, his blue eyes are shadowed and creased, but he looks more worried than angry. My stomach starts to hurt. "I don't use drugs. We weren't at a party or anything like that."

Mom still looks skeptical. "Then..."

I take a deep breath. "Parker and I have these friends— well, we *had* these friends—that were talking about doing something really stupid. We wanted to try to stop them. To talk them out of it. I thought they'd listen to us. That's why I went out. And Parker—well, she needs to get away from them, but she can't go back to her parents' house, so I was hoping she could stay here. You know, for a few days. Until she figures something out."

"You're not making sense," Mom says. Her voice is sharp with anxiety. "What were you doing tonight? The *truth*, Emily."

The truth. I look at my parents, and realize I have to tell them. The fire is going to be on the news; the school will probably be closed; we smell like smoke. They're not stupid. They're going to connect the dots. I look at my Dad and my throat starts getting all tight and achy so it's hard to talk. "These guys we know...they were talking about starting a fire. At the high school." I don't know why but for some reason I start to cry. "I'm sorry. I thought we could stop them."

My parents both stare at me like they're in shock. Tears are blurring my vision and I blink, tasting salt at the back of my throat. "We went to the high school to try to stop them," I say. I try to take a deep breath, but it comes out as a series of gasps.

Mom's eyes are wide and her mouth is hanging slightly open. "You did...you went...These boys started a fire? You were involved in *arson*?"

"I wasn't exactly involved," I say. "I mean, I didn't help or anything. I thought we could talk them out of it."

Mom pulls her housecoat tighter around herself. She opens her mouth and shuts it again, as if she doesn't even know where to begin.

Parker grabs my hand beneath the table and squeezes it for a second before she lets go again. Even though I know she means nothing by it, I just about choke.

"One of the guys wanted to stop," she says. "But not Jamie.

He wouldn't listen to us. We couldn't do anything."

There is a very long silence. Finally, Mom looks at Dad and Dad looks at me. "Are you saying these boys you know actually started a fire at the school?" he asks.

I nod miserably. "One of them. Yes. We called the fire department."

Dad gets up and switches on the tiny kitchen TV to the local news channel. Some guy with a toupee is talking about a dog show. He turns the volume down low but leaves the TV on.

"I don't understand why you didn't talk to me," Mom says. "If you were worried about these boys doing this, why keep it all a secret and sneak out in the middle of the night?"

Hearing her say it like that makes it sound so stupid. I shrug. "I don't know why. I didn't really think of it, I guess."

"You didn't think of it," she repeats slowly. "You knew these boys were planning to start a fire at the school, and it didn't occur to you to tell an adult? It didn't even cross your mind that it might be a good idea?"

I shake my head. "I didn't think they'd really do it, I guess. I didn't want to get them in trouble."

"Well, I'd say they've got themselves into some real trouble now," she says grimly.

Dad waves his hands at us. "Shh, shh." He turns up the volume on the TV and we all look over to see a picture of fire trucks in front of GRSS. I can't tell from the picture what's happening or if the fire is out.

"…fire at Glen Ridge Secondary School appears to have been set deliberately," a reporter is saying. She is standing in front of GRSS, holding a microphone, her hair sprayed into a shiny helmet. "A young male was arrested fleeing the scene and is facing charges related to arson. Thanks to a report from an observant neighbor, firefighters were on the scene quickly and were able to prevent the fire from spreading. However, they say the damage to the rear wing of the school is significant and that the school may be closed for some time. We will keep you updated with more information, including the identity of the suspect and plans for GRSS students, as it becomes available."

I watch as the image of GRSS on the screen disappears. Leo must have got away then. So I guess we accomplished something by going to the school. I can't believe Jamie got caught. I thought for sure he'd be gone before anyone got to the school. He had plenty of time to get away. For a second I wonder if he'll rat Leo out and try to share the blame—but much as I dislike Jamie, I'm pretty sure he won't do that.

Mostly what I'm feeling is relief: I'm so glad Parker wasn't with them.

I turn and look at her. Her eyes are wide and scared, and her face is as white as her hair. I wonder if she's thinking the same thing. Maybe she's just upset. She's still in love with Jamie, after all, and she's probably wondering what's going to happen now.

"Mom? Can Parker stay with us? Please, just until she figures out what to do?"

My mother looks at my father.

He clears his throat. "Parker, where is your own family?"

"I haven't lived with them for a while." Her voice isn't much more than a whisper. "I have my own place though. I guess I probably should have gone there tonight. If you want me to go…" She stands up.

"No, we don't," I say quickly.

Mom frowns at me. "Dante. No one's saying your friend has to leave. We're just trying to…to understand."

"Sorry." I look at Parker. "But Parker…you can't go back there."

"It's my home, Dante."

"But your parents…," Mom says. "Surely if they knew you needed help…"

Parker shrugs. "You'd think. But things were pretty bad at home. Besides, I have a job. It's not like, you know, I'm on the streets or anything."

"You're not in school?" Mom's eyebrows shoot up even higher, wrinkling her forehead into a hundred fine lines. *Avoid excessive facial expressions*, I think, and suppress a totally inappropriate giggle.

Parker sits back down slowly. "I left part way through grade ten."

Mom shakes her head. "Well, if you're going to stay here, you'll have to go to school."

"I'll only be here for a couple of days," Parker says stiffly. "Like I told you, I have my own place."

"I'll have to talk to your parents," Mom says. "They should at least know where you are."

I look at Parker anxiously, but she's nodding. "I'll call them in the morning," she says. "You can talk to them." She smiles tentatively at my mom; then she suddenly bursts into tears like a little kid. "Thank you so, so much," she says, her voice all choked up. "I can't believe, after all this, you're going to let me stay here."

My parents look at each other for a long minute, doing that silent communication thing, and then Dad says, "Well. We'll see how it goes."

"Thank you so much," I say, blinking tears away again. "I knew you guys wouldn't turn her out, no matter how mad you were at me. You're the best."

He meets my eyes for a moment and then looks down at the table. "We've always trusted you, Dante. And you've always been a private kid." He gives a half-grin, half-grimace. "Like me that way, I guess. Not a big talker." He looks up again and this time holds my gaze with his. "But it is easier to respect someone's privacy if you can trust them to talk to you when they need to."

I don't think I've ever heard him make such a long speech. I swallow hard. "I know. I'm really sorry."

He and Mom look at each other again; then Mom looks at me. "Parker can stay in the spare room, Emily. It's all made up." She looks at her watch. "Well, my goodness," she says brightly. "Look at the time! We'd better all go to bed."

Conversation over, or—more likely—to be continued.

TWENTY-TWO

I show Parker to the spare room, but a few minutes later, she's tapping lightly at my bedroom door. I jump up and let her in, and close the door quietly behind us.

"I'm so wide awake," she whispers. "It's practically morning. Are you going to be able to sleep?"

"Probably not, but my parents..." I don't want to get in more trouble for having her in my room. I feel guilty enough already.

"Your parents are amazing."

"Yeah. They're pretty okay." I sit down on the edge of my bed.

Parker sits down beside me, legs crossed. "I can't believe Jamie got caught," she whispers. Her eyes are suddenly glistening like she's holding back tears. "Dante? If you hadn't come and got me tonight...I'd have been there with them, you know. I'd have been caught too. So... well, I guess I owe you."

"You don't owe me anything," I say quickly.

"I do though." She puts her hand on my arm. "Thanks, Dante. I don't think I've ever had a friend like you before. I mean, I feel like I can count on you, you know?"

Now, I think. *Tell her.* "Parker?" I draw in a long uneven breath.

"Mmm?"

Her hand is still resting on my arm, her fingers soft and cool against my skin. I can smell the smoke on her hair. "Um, you can. Count on me, I mean." I clear my throat. "I...look, I should tell you something. I really...I love you, Parker."

"I love you too," she says softly. "You're the best friend I've ever had."

I shake my head and pull my arm away. "No. I mean, I really love you. I'm in love with you."

She stares at me, and I can see the uncertainty flickering across her face. "Um, you mean..."

"I mean, Jamie wasn't wrong. About me." I hate that I'm bringing Jamie into this, letting him of all people be the one to name what I am, but I can't quite say it. And I don't know what word to use. Queer? I haven't used the word out loud before, not about myself anyway. Gay? Or is that only for men? Lesbian sounds so...clinical. I don't like that word. I don't like any of the words.

"You mean...," Parker says again.

I clench my teeth for a second; then I spit it out. "I mean, I'm queer."

There's an awkward silence and I stare down at my hands.

"Oh. I didn't...I didn't know." Parker's voice is soft and careful. "Uh, Dante? I love you too, you know that, right?"

My heart lifts for a second and flutters like a pair of wings in my chest. Then I look at her, and she drops her gaze, and my heart stops fluttering. It drops like a bird that's been shot from the sky.

"It's just, I'm not...well, you know." She can't even say it. "But...well, we can still be friends, right?"

"Course we can," I say. My cheeks are burning. I don't know what I expected. "I just...I mean, I know you're straight. I just had to tell you. I hope I didn't make you too uncomfortable."

There's a pause and then Parker giggles. "I'm kind of flattered, actually." She's smiling a little, her pale cheeks flushed pink. "You know. That you're attracted to me."

I want her to stop talking about it. I want her to leave. "Whatever. It's no big thing."

"You really do mean a lot to me," she says. "You know, as a friend."

"Yeah." I gesture to the door. "I guess you'd better go back to your room. I don't want to push my luck. With my parents, I mean."

She stands up as if she's going to leave; then she quickly bends down and kisses me, fast and hard, on the lips. "Night, Dante."

I try to catch my breath. "Night," I whisper. I watch her go; then I flop back down on my bed. What the fuck? That wasn't just a friendly kiss, if there is such a thing. I can still feel the heat of her lips on mine.

Of course, I'm awake half the night. My mind runs in the same old circles until I feel like a hamster on a spinning wheel. Parker, Jamie, my parents, Leo, Parker, the school, Parker, Parker, Parker. What was I thinking, telling her how I felt? What could have made me think that was a good idea? And most of all, I'm wondering what the hell that kiss was supposed to mean. What was she thinking, kissing me like that, right after she finished her whole *I love you as a friend* spiel?

I feel guilty—disloyal—for thinking this way, but I feel like she was messing with my head. Not on purpose, maybe, but still. I can't believe I'm thinking this—I would have said I'd give anything to kiss Parker—but I almost wish she hadn't done that.

Then again, maybe she really does like me.

I guess I eventually drift off to sleep, because the next thing I know it's morning and Mom is standing in my doorway.

"Dante?"

"Mmmpphh?"

"I have to go to work in a few minutes."

"Oh." I sit up. "Okay."

She steps closer, stands just inside my door with one hand resting on my dresser. "I wanted to talk to you before I go. Before your friend wakes up."

I blink a few times. My mouth tastes like ashes. "Was there more on the news this morning? Is there school today?"

"No. They're talking about bussing kids to a couple of different schools during the repairs, but they haven't figured out details. I bet it'll be Monday before you're back at school."

"Oh." I rub my face with the palms of my hands. "Mom? Thanks for last night. For being so…understanding."

She shakes her head. "I don't understand the first thing about this."

"Well. You know, for letting Parker stay."

"I could hardly turn her out, could I?" She lowers her voice. "The boy who was arrested. Is that her boyfriend?"

I nod. "He's an ass—I mean, a jerk."

"Yes."

There is a pause. I figure Mom probably has all kinds of questions, but I hope she doesn't want to get into it right now. I'm barely awake.

"Were you trying to help her, Emily? Is that why you got involved in all this?"

It'd be easy to just agree. It's the only possible explanation that could make me look at least a little bit good in her eyes. It'd be way easier than trying to tell the truth: Right now, I don't even know what the truth is. I shake my head. "I don't know. I don't know, Mom." Next thing I know, my throat's all tight and my eyes are hot and then I'm starting to cry.

Mom doesn't rush over to comfort me though. She just stands there, looking really tired, and she slowly shakes her head. "I thought I knew you better than this. I would've sworn up and down that you had far too much common sense to get mixed up with a bad crowd."

I don't say anything. I can't think of a single thing to say.

"I'd like to help your friend, honey, but…well, I don't want to see her drag you down. She seems sweet enough, but it's pretty obvious that she's got some big problems."

Then I hear Parker's voice right outside my door. "Don't worry," she says. "I won't be staying."

Mom turns, her face startled and guilty. "Goodness, you made me jump." Her forehead creases. "Oh dear. I hope I haven't upset you."

"That's okay." Parker's voice is stiff and she isn't looking at me or my mom. "I have to get home anyway."

I scramble out of bed. "Parker, it's okay. You don't have to go."

She shakes her head. "I guess I'll talk to you later."

And that's it. Just like that, she's gone. I don't say anything until I hear the front door slam shut. Then I turn to my mother. "Nice going, Mom. Happy now?"

"That's not fair," she protests. "I didn't mean for her to hear me."

"Are you sure about that?" A part of me knows I'm being unreasonable, that what I'm saying isn't totally accurate, but I can't stop myself. "Because it sure was convenient, wasn't it? She's gone, and you get to pretend it's not your fault at all."

She tugs her cardigan down and smoothes the knitted fabric over her hips. "I told her she was welcome to stay."

My voice is getting louder. "Yeah, and then you called her messed up."

"I didn't say that."

"Oh right. You just said she had big problems. Totally different."

"Drop the sarcasm." Mom steps inside my room. Her face is pink and two white lines have appeared by her nostrils, always a sure sign that she's seriously pissed off. "That's enough. You are in plenty of trouble already, don't you think? Sneaking out at night to hang out with a bunch of...a bunch of *delinquents*...I swear, Emily, I don't know what I've done to deserve this kind of..." She breaks off and shakes her head, lips pressed together in a thin hard line.

"This kind of daughter? Is that what you were going to say? Because it's totally obvious that's how you feel. You didn't get the kind of daughter you wanted. You didn't get a pretty, perfect little girl who just wants to fit in, no matter what."

She shakes her head and doesn't say anything for a minute. Then she takes a deep breath, loud enough that I can actually hear her do it. "Emily..."

"I'm not Emily," I yell. "I'm not Emily and I *can't* be Emily, okay? So...so..." My voice is suddenly choked with tears, but I can't cry—I refuse to cry—so I just stop talking and try to swallow despite the knife-like pain in my throat.

There's a long silence. I stare down at my bedspread and watch the colors swim in a blur of soft pastel. My heart is pounding, and I don't know what to say. I'm not even sure exactly what we are fighting about. Nothing. Everything. I keep hearing the sound of Parker's feet running down the hall and the front door slamming behind her. Running back to Jamie.

"I just don't understand why you didn't talk to me," Mom says at last. "About these boys or about your friend and her problems. Why do you always feel like you have to deal with everything on your own?"

She doesn't sound angry anymore. She sounds sort of defeated, and I am suddenly flooded with guilt. I rub my hands over my eyes and look up at her. "Mom..."

She ignores me. "You never did tell me anything, even when you were little. You always said everything was fine, and then I'd find out from your teacher that you were getting teased, or that you'd fallen and hurt yourself, or whatever. I used to think you didn't trust me. Is that it? Is that why you snuck out in the night instead of coming to us?"

"It's not about you," I tell her. "I just didn't think of it."

She sighs. "That's what your dad always told me when you were small too. That you were just too damn independent to ask for help."

I can't believe she just said "damn." She never swears.

Neither of us says anything for a minute. It's not like we've resolved anything; it's more like we both just ran out of energy for fighting, or maybe we realized there was no point to it. Finally she shrugs. "I have to go to work," she says.

I've agreed to spend the day studying. It goes without saying that I'm grounded.

I try to work on my English paper, the one about Tess. It's basically done. It just needs a conclusion, a snappy ending, something to sum it all up. And I can't think of one. It's all too complicated to explain in a few neat lines. Besides, I can't concentrate. All I can think about is Parker: how she seemed when I first met her, all cocky and sure of herself; the way she always said what she thought; the way she acted as if no challenge was insurmountable; the way she seemed to believe we could do anything, change anything, as long as we threw ourselves into it hard enough; the way she didn't believe in brick walls.

I know Mom sees her as messed up because she doesn't go to school and doesn't live at home, but that isn't how I see it. I think that Parker just got dealt a lousy hand and that she did what she needed to do to get through it all. She made choices that were right for her. But Jamie…that's a choice I can't understand. I can't see it as a good thing, even though Parker says it was. I picture her quick grin and the way her skin crinkles around her eyes when she laughs. How can someone be so smart and so together, and yet so screwed up, all at the same time?

I spend half the morning on the Internet, reading. *Teens and Dating Violence. Understanding the Cycle of Abuse. Is someone you know in an Abusive Relationship? Spot the Warning Signs.* I read about power and control and gender stereotypes and intergenerational patterns. I read about low self-esteem, about post-traumatic stress, about denial. I read that girls stay with abusive guys because they are scared to leave, because they think the abuse is a sign of love, because they think the guy will change, because they don't have healthy role models, because they are socially isolated, because the abuse has eroded their self-confidence and ability to trust their own judgment.

In the end, I shut my laptop and stare out the window. It all makes sense and none of it makes sense. None of it is enough to help me understand Parker.

TWENTY-THREE

I'm still sitting there, sort of thinking and sort of drifting, when the doorbell rings. *Parker.* I run down the stairs two at a time, slide the dead bolt and throw the front door open.

It's Leo. He shifts from one foot to the other like he's not quite sure what he's doing here. "I figured you'd probably be home. Not at school, I mean."

No shit. "You want to come in?" I say, stepping back a little.

He follows me to the kitchen. I grab a couple cans of Coke—Dad's big vice—and sit down at the table. "So."

"Yeah." He takes a can from me and opens it. *Click-tttssss.* The noise seems too loud in this big silent house. "I guess you heard? About Jamie?"

"Uh-huh. Is he…?" I don't know what I'm asking. Is he in jail, I guess. I don't know how these things work. "Is he back home then? Or…"

"Yeah, he's home. He's got a court date when he has to appear." Leo tilts his head back and drinks; his Adam's apple bobs up and down in his skinny throat.

"Jeez."

"I know." He sets the can on the table in front of him and lifts it up and down a few times, moving it around, making a pattern of intersecting wet circles on the glass surface of the table. "I guess I should say thanks. If you and Parker hadn't showed up...I mean, I'd probably have got busted too. Would've killed my parents, you know? And they don't have the money to hire some fancy lawyer."

"Do Jamie's?"

He nods. "They already have, according to Parker."

His eyes are locked onto mine in that way he has, that intense gaze Parker used to tease him about. Used to. Everything feels like it's in past tense now. I clear my throat. "It all got kind of fucked up, didn't it? What happened, Leo?"

"I don't know. I've been asking myself that same thing." He hasn't shaved, and in the sunlight streaming through the windows I can see the glint of blondish brown stubble across his cheeks and chin. "After you climbed your school that night, and we talked about GRSS and Mr. Lawson and all that stuff, it got me thinking. Remembering things that happened a few years ago."

I nod. I know about it from Linnea, but I don't want to tell him that.

He drops his gaze, spins the Coke can around and almost spills it. "Shit." He sets it back upright. "It wasn't a good time for me."

"That's okay, Leo. I mean, you don't have to talk about it if you don't…"

"I should've told you," he says. "If I'd told you, maybe I wouldn't have ended up spilling it all to Jamie just because we had a few drinks."

"Is that what happened?"

"Yeah. And he was all sympathetic. Man, he's a chameleon, that guy. He was all *Yeah man, that totally sucks, have another drink.* Then next thing I know, he's like *Let's burn the fucker down.*"

"GRSS."

He nods. "I should've walked away. I don't know why I didn't."

"He was your friend," I say.

"Yeah." He traces a wet line on the table with one finger. "And when I tried to say it maybe wasn't a good idea, he just threw it all back in my face. All the stuff I'd told him."

I swallow hard. Guessing. Knowing. "He called you a fag."

"Yeah." He looks straight at me. "I'm not queer, you know. But I used to get that shit a lot when I was a kid. Beat up, called names. I don't know why."

"Leo?"

"Yeah."

"I am. Queer, I mean." It's easier to say this time.

His eyebrows lift but he doesn't look away, not even for a second. "Yeah? Shit. I didn't know that."

"No. Well, I haven't exactly told a lot of people."

Then he laughs. "Guess maybe I shouldn't have kissed you that night then."

"That's okay. If I liked guys, you'd probably be the kind of guy I'd like. If that makes any sense."

"I guess that's a compliment, right? To be honest, I haven't had much luck with relationships lately." He pulls a baggie out of his pocket and starts rolling a joint right there on my mom's kitchen table. "Mainly because I've spent the last year totally hung up on someone who's determined to waste her life being in love with an asshole."

"Um, you can't smoke in here," I say. Then I realize what he's just said. "Sorry. Delayed hearing. Are you talking about…?"

"Parker? Yeah. She's the main reason I've stuck around." He licks the rolling paper. "I've been a fucking idiot. Just been kidding myself, I guess."

I stare at him. I don't know whether to laugh or cry.

He holds the joint up. "Can we go in your backyard or something?"

I nod and get up, lead the way through the house and out the sliding glass doors and sit down beside him on the back steps. Out of sight of the neighbors, hopefully. "Leo?"

"Yeah." He lights up and squints at me through the smoke.

The smoke wafts my way, and it is definitely not tobacco. I glance over toward the house next door. Hopefully everyone is at work. "You meant what you said back there? About how you feel about Parker?"

Leo nods. "Can't help it. Waste of my time, obviously.

When you came along..." He breaks off and laughs. "Well, you know what they say."

"What?"

"The best way to get over someone is to get on top of someone else."

I give a startled laugh. Sometimes I think I'm almost as uptight as my mother.

"Sorry. I was just kidding, but I guess that was a bit crass."

"No, it's okay. I get it."

"I liked you, Dante. I mean, I still do. I thought we had a good connection, you know? But Parker...Shit. I don't know what it is about her."

"I know."

"Yeah." He takes a drag and taps the ash off into the tidily mowed green grass.

"Leo?" I swallow nervously. My heart is racing and my hands are wet, but I have to talk to someone about her. "I mean, I really do know. About Parker. I kind of...well, I kind of feel the same way about her."

He nods slowly like that doesn't surprise him at all. Like he figures anyone who knew Parker would feel the same way. He leans down, butts out the joint on the ground and carefully puts the little papery end bit into his pocket. "Did you tell her?" he asks at last.

"Yeah." My cheeks are hot. "Last night."

"Was she cool with it?"

I thought about it. "Pretty cool. I guess. She didn't freak out or anything."

"But…"

"Yeah. She's straight. She's with Jamie. I'm an idiot for thinking anything else."

Leo puts his arm around me and gives me a sideways hug. "I'm sorry. Of course, if you managed to get anywhere with her, I'd probably have to kill you. But…I really am sorry. If I had to pick, I'd rather see her with you than Jamie." He sighs. "Unrequited love. It sucks."

"She kissed me." I blurt it out. I don't know why I feel like I have to tell him this, but I want to come clean. It's like we're in this together now, in a weird way. Parker is so out of our reach that we're not even competition for each other—we're just fellow sufferers.

"No shit?" He pulls back and looks at me. For a second I think maybe I shouldn't have told him. Then he shakes his head slowly. I can see a muscle in his jaw tighten and release, tighten and release. "I don't want to sound like I'm bad-mouthing her. I'm crazy about Parker, you know that. Right?"

"Yeah." I want to know where he's going with this.

"I went over there one time, months and months ago. She and Jamie had been fighting. She was alone, crying and freaking out." He shrugs. "We had a few drinks. I told her how I felt about her. It was dumb, I guess, but I was hoping she and Jamie were through. I was hoping if she knew how I felt…" He shrugs again, lifting his skinny shoulders and dropping them like the weight is too much. "I wanted to take care of her, you know?"

"Yeah." *God, do I ever.*

"Next thing I know...well." He looks down at his feet, crosses one ankle over the other.

I notice that he's wearing hiking boots. Beat-up, old, Timberland Gore-Tex hiking boots, same as mine. "She kissed you?"

"Yeah."

"More than that? More than kissing?"

He frowns. "Dante..."

"Sorry." I don't really want to know anyway. "And then what happened?"

"Nothing."

"Nothing?"

"I left before Jamie came home." He looks at me to make sure I'm understanding correctly. "Not because I wanted to. Because she told me to, Dante. And the next time I saw her, she acted like nothing happened. Picked back up with Jamie." Leo pulls out a pack of tobacco and starts rolling a cigarette. "I should've known, right?"

"No. She shouldn't have done that. Not knowing how you felt. It wasn't fair." *She shouldn't have kissed me either.* That's what I'm thinking.

He sighs and offers me the cigarette. I shake my head automatically. "Right," he says. "You're a runner. Clean lungs. I remember." He sticks it in his mouth, lights up and inhales. "The thing is, I don't think she means to hurt anyone when she does that shit."

"No. I know. Jeez, Leo. You don't have to tell me."

He narrows his eyes and looks at me. "I've basically given up. I know it's never going to go anywhere. But you…well, you've got it bad, don't you?"

His streaky hair is falling around his face like a mane. Leo, lion, loyal. "I guess so," I say. "I guess I do."

He gives a slow, not entirely friendly grin. "And she knows it, my friend. And you better remember that."

TWENTY-FOUR

Parker doesn't call me all day Wednesday or Thursday, and of course she doesn't have a phone so I can't call her. Friday morning after Mom and Dad leave for work, I break down and call Leo.

"Have you seen her? Is she okay?"

"Depends what you mean by okay."

"Leo...come on."

He sighs. "I was over there last night. Jamie's pretty pissed at me for taking off."

"If you hadn't, you'd both have been caught," I protest. "Anyway, he could've stopped too. It's not your fault he didn't."

"Yeah. But...I don't know, Dante. I don't think I'm going to be hanging out there so much anymore." He clears his throat. "Time to move on."

"What about Parker?"

"What about her?"

I try to remember her exact words. "You know what she told me once? She told me you were the kind of guy who wouldn't let a girl down, you know? The kind of guy who'd always be there."

Leo gives a short, bitter laugh. "Yeah. Well, apparently that isn't the kind of guy she wants."

"I think she really loves you. As a friend, Leo."

"Yeah. So she says. No offence, Dante, but the whole *I-love-you-as-a-friend* thing was getting a little tired. If you can do it, more power to you."

"Don't walk away from her, Leo. She needs us." I feel like I might start crying.

"Aww, come on. I'm not saying I won't take her calls, okay? Just that the ball's in her court. I'm not going over there so that Jamie can call me a faggot and Parker can flirt with me whenever he's out of the room."

I picture Parker sitting on the living room floor, crying, that night she and Jamie fought. I remember the way she jumped up when Leo came to the door. I guess any hint of a crack in her blind loyalty to Jamie is a good thing, but still, I don't like to think about her flirting with Leo. I push the thought aside. "You think Jamie will go to jail? I looked up the penalties for arson and criminal mischief and all that stuff…it's pretty bad."

"Dunno. He's convinced this hotshot lawyer is going to get him off. But maybe he'll do some time. Maybe that'll give Parker the break she needs to get away."

"So you do still care about her," I say, like I've caught him out.

"Of course I care about her."

"If you see her...could you give her a message for me? Just tell her I hope...I hope she's okay?"

"Tell her yourself," he says. "You'll see her tonight, right?"

Social Skills 101. I'd completely forgotten. "Is she going?"

"You know what, Dante? Parker makes fun of that group, but I'll tell you something. She never misses it. Never."

As soon as Mom gets home, I raise the subject carefully. All our conversations have been a bit careful and awkward since that stupid fight. "I have that group tonight, Mom. I know I'm grounded but...If it's okay, I'd like to go."

She slips her jacket off, carefully arranges it on a hanger and puts it in the coat closet. "Why? To see that girl?"

I might as well be honest, because she's not going to believe I'd go for any other reason. "Yes. Mom, I know you think she's messed up..." I take a deep breath. "And I guess she is, sort of. Her boyfriend is an abusive jerk and she can't seem to...I don't know. She's sort of...caught." I look at my mom and will her to understand. "But she needs her friends to stick by her. She needs me."

Mom nods slowly. "I don't know, Dante. Let me think about it. Let me talk to your dad."

Mom's in the middle of making dinner when Dad gets home, so I decide to get a word in with him first. I follow him to his office in the basement and stand there while he unpacks papers from his briefcase.

"What's up?" he asks.

"Dad?"

He puts down his bag and turns to look at me. His forehead's all lined and worried-looking, like one of those wrinkly dogs, and I suddenly feel all emotional, as if I might start bawling for no reason at all. It's all been too much, these last few days.

"You okay, honey?"

I sniff a little and blink hard, but it's no good. I'm all choked up. I can't even talk.

The wrinkles deepen. "What is it? What's wrong?" He sounds scared. I guess the whole fire thing was probably a pretty big shock. He's probably wondering what else he doesn't know about me. And that thought starts me crying even harder.

"Honey…please tell me." He reaches out one arm tentatively, like he isn't sure whether I'll accept a hug or not.

I let myself lean against him and he wraps his arms around me tightly. He smells like coffee and aftershave, and he feels so solid. "I'm okay," I say. I wonder what he'd say if I told him how I feel about Parker. If I told him about Beth.

"We love you so much," he says. "I wish you'd talk to us." He goes all quiet, but not like he's distracted or thinking about something else. Just quiet in a waiting kind of way, like he's just leaving room for me to talk.

I imagine saying it: *Dad, I think I'm queer.* I close my eyes for a second. I can't do it. I can't tell him. I feel like I have to say something though, like his silence is creating a vacuum and the words are getting sucked right out of me. "Dad?"

"Yes." He leans away from me slightly so that he can see my face.

"Um. Um." I think I'd find it easier to confess that I have a skull tattoo, or a crack addiction, or that I've found Jesus. None of which is true, fortunately. But this…It's not that I think he couldn't handle it. Even Mom would probably be okay: She'd worry about what people would think but she'd get over it. It wouldn't change the way she feels about me.

This just feels too personal to share. Eventually I'll tell them. But I don't think it'll be anytime soon. "I love you too," I tell him.

Technically, being grounded means no Internet, but I go up to my bedroom and go online anyway. I don't understand how I can feel so guilty about hurting my parents, and at the same time, keep disregarding their rules. I just feel like I need to do this. If they understood, they wouldn't mind. If they really understood, they'd want me to do what I needed to do. But maybe I'm deluding myself and just making excuses to do whatever I want. I don't know.

For the first time in ages, I go to Beth's Facebook page. I don't check to see who all her new friends are, or even bother reading the updates in her profile. I just look at her picture for a long minute and wait to see how I feel. Nothing much. A little sad, maybe, but in a detached, nostalgic kind of way, like it all happened a long time ago. I don't feel any urge to write to her anymore.

Then I search for Linnea. I don't know if she's even on Facebook, but there she is: Her last name is Zukanovic, so she's not exactly hard to find. I send her a friend request with a message attached: *Hey Linnea, About that group? Count me in.*

At dinner, Mom tells me that I can go to the Social Skills group after all. "I know you're grounded, but I think you need to talk to someone, and maybe this counselor will be able to help you to…well, to get some perspective on things."

I picture Shelley's earnest face and her scented markers. "Maybe," I say. "Uh, Mom? Thanks. For letting me go anyway. Thanks a lot."

"Your dad will drop you off," she says. "And I'll pick you up. I'll be waiting outside when you come out."

I hate that I've made them worry like this. I hate it. "I'll be there," I promise.

Dad's not as concerned about punctuality as Mom, so we roll up to the church just as the group is due to start.

"Off you go then, honey."

"Dad?"

"Yeah?"

"Thanks."

He shakes his head like there's nothing to thank him for. "Go on." He winks at me. "Get in there and teach 'em some social skills."

TWENTY-FIVE

As I walk down the stairs, my hands start sweating. I realize I'm nervous about seeing Parker. I'm worried that she'll be cool and standoffish, that things will be awkward and different between us. I take a deep breath, run my hands through my hair and enter the room.

They're all there, sitting in a circle on those uncomfortable wooden chairs in the middle of the too-big room. Parker's face lights up when she sees me. "Dante! You made it!"

I grin at her, instantly flooded with relief. She's wearing her hair tied back in a ponytail, which makes her face look even skinnier, and the same old jeans and striped sweater. The first couple of times I met her, I thought that sweater was her favorite—sort of her trademark look. Now I figure maybe it's the only one she owns.

Shelley smiles at me. "Welcome, Dante. Good to see you again. We're just starting check-in."

"Oh." I sit down in the empty chair between Parker—was she saving it for me?—and Nicki. "Is it my turn?"

"Sure, why don't you go next? For today, we're just saying one thing we each hope to take away from this group."

At least it makes sense, for once. At least I don't have to describe anything metaphorically as one of the four seasons. I look around the group and wonder who all these girls really are and how we all ended up sitting here in this basement together.

"Something you want to take away?" Shelley prompts.

Other than Parker, I guess. "Um. Can I think about that for a minute?"

"As much time as you need."

It's hard to think when six girls are staring at you, especially when one of them is Parker. I choose my words carefully. "Okay. The thing is, I guess we all want to change some things in our lives, right?"

Everyone is nodding, except Nicki, who is lifting one lip in a sneer, probably because she thinks I'm kissing up to Shelley. Which I am not. "Um, okay. And I think it's good to talk about how we feel and all that, but…" I look right at Parker. "But sometimes I think you have to take some action too, you know? I mean, to really make things change." *Like, leave your asshole boyfriend.*

Shelley frowns. "Change is internal, Dante. It comes from within. Learning to feel better about yourself, accepting yourself as you are."

"Right. Sure." I actually feel okay about myself already. "But some things outside yourself might need to change too. So maybe we could talk about that. About what to do about the things you can't just accept."

"You don't always have a choice," Parker says flatly.

"One at a time," Shelley says. "Parker, you're next. Can you hold that thought until it's your turn to speak?"

"I'm done," I say quickly. "Over to you, Parker."

She shrugs. "I've got nothing to say."

Shelley waits for a minute, but Parker just stares at the floor.

At break, Parker and I head outdoors and sit down on the cement barrier that edges the parking lot. She takes out a cigarette, lights up and exhales a long stream of smoke into the night air. Then she tilts her head back and looks at me through narrowed eyes. "So."

"So," I say.

"If that comment about changing things was aimed at me, I didn't really appreciate it."

"Oh come on," I say. "You're all about changing school systems and governments, but when it comes to our own lives, we have to accept whatever crap we're dealt? That's bullshit, Parker."

She smokes in silence for a minute. I don't know if she's seriously pissed off or just thinking. I wait awhile, but she still doesn't say anything, and I don't have my dad's patience. "I guess you and Jamie got back together then," I say eventually.

"We never really broke up," she says, shrugging. "He's pretty pissed at me though. Like everything that happened was my fault. So we're not really talking."

"What are you going to do?"

Parker doesn't answer. She takes a drag, and the end of her cigarette glows in the darkness. She looks at the ash, just stares at it for a minute as if she might find the answer there. Usually she smokes her cigarettes right to the filter, holding them right at the base of her fingers like she's trying to hide them or shelter them from the rain; but she tosses this one to the ground only half-smoked.

"I don't know what to do," she says. She slides closer to me and rests her head on my shoulder. "What do you think I should do? What would you do?"

Her hair is silk against my neck and smells like green apples. It's all I can do not to bury my face in it. I sit still, barely breathing. "You know what I think," I say, trying to keep my voice steady. "I think you should get the hell out. But...well, it's not up to me, is it?"

"See...that's what I like about you," Parker whispers. "I bet it'd be so different to be with someone like you. You'd never tell me what to do, would you, Dante? If I was your girlfriend?"

God, I'm so crazy about her and I'm thinking, *maybe, just maybe...* Then I hear Leo's voice in my head—*She knows it, my friend*—and I pull away. "What are you doing, Parker?" I ask her. My voice sounds colder than I mean it to.

She lifts her head and looks at me. "What do you mean?"

I don't want to fight with her. Besides, part of my brain is still saying maybe she really could like me that way; maybe it's possible; maybe she's not all that straight after all. So I just shake my head. "Nothing. Forget it."

"What'd I do? Are you mad at me?"

Leo's voice is in my head again. *Flirting with me when-ever Jamie's out of the room.* Is that what she's doing? "Nothing," I say. "It's fine."

Her husky blue eyes are suddenly shining, blinking. "I wasn't messing with you," she says. "I wouldn't do that."

"Yeah." She's so close I can hear her breathing, so close I can smell the sweet apple scent of her shampoo. "It's okay, Parker."

She looks like she might start crying. "You're mad, aren't you?"

I wish I was. It might be easier. "Nope. Not mad."

Parker bites her lip. "I'm sorry. I guess I was being a bit..." She gestures in frustration. "I sort of wish I felt that way. About you, I mean."

"But you don't."

She shakes her head. "No. And you know, there's Jamie."

"Right," I say. "There's Jamie. Okay then."

"Okay." Her voice is sad. "We'll always be friends, right?"

"Yes," I tell her. I hope it's the truth.

The next morning I wake insanely early. The house is still and silent and dark, but I can't imagine going back to sleep. I lie there for a few minutes, feeling oddly peaceful and not really thinking about anything; then I get out of bed, pull on my sweats and tiptoe down the carpeted stairs. I scrawl a quick note on the whiteboard in the kitchen, just in case Mom wakes up before I get back. *Gone for a run, back soon, love D.*

The air is cold and dry, and it's not even close to light out. Big black sky and wide empty roads and the smell of autumn. I stand at the end of my driveway, lacing my runners and doing a few quick stretches. Then I start to run, my feet landing sure and light on the smooth asphalt, my breathing easy, my legs strong, my heart pumping a steady rhythm. Times like this, I think I could run forever.

When I get to GRSS, I slow down. In the darkness, I can't see the damage. Not from the road, anyway. Across the field, the school sits there solidly, a gray indestructible-looking mass. In a few weeks, it'll be fixed up and we'll all be back in those corridors, and everything will, I suppose, go on as usual. I let my fingers brush against one of the spindly trees as I run past; then I pick up my pace again and leave the school behind.

It seems odd that more hasn't changed after every-thing that has happened in these last few weeks. You'd think there'd be more visible signs. I remember Jamie's arm lifting and the bottle flying through the air in a slow-motion arc, flames exploding from the classroom window. *This is for you. Watch it burn. Dante's fucking inferno.*

I don't think I'll be spending time with Jamie again, and much as I don't want to believe it, I don't think Parker is going to leave him. Not anytime soon. And I don't know what this means for our friendship. I'm not walking away and I'll be there for her if she asks for help, but I won't put my life on hold. I'm not going to torture myself. It sounds as hokey as something Shelley would say, but I have to move on. Whatever that means.

These last few weeks have been a crazy kind of journey, but even though it ended up in such an ugly mess, I wouldn't want to undo it all. The world looks different to me now, like something has shifted, like the lenses I'm looking through have changed. More things seem possible now. I tilt my head back and look up at the sky. It's not quite black after all—more of a deep purple-gray—and it's filled with tiny points of light. I find myself thinking of the last line of the *Inferno*, as Dante emerges from hell: *And we walked out once more beneath the stars.*

Of course, for him the stars were the stars of heaven, and I don't believe in heaven any more than I believe in hell.

Still, they're awfully beautiful.

ACKNOWLEDGMENTS

Many thanks to everyone who read and gave thoughtful feedback on various versions of this story. I am especially grateful to Gwyneth Evans, Debra Henry, Cheryl May, Michelle Mulder, Holly Phillips, Pat Schmatz and Ilse Stevenson for their insight, inspiration and support. Thanks also to my amazing editor Sarah Harvey and the fabulous team at Orca.

Robin Stevenson is the author of several novels for teens, including *A Thousand Shades of Blue* and *Out of Order*. She lives in Victoria, British Columbia. More information about Robin and her books is available on her website at www.robinstevenson.com.